中课程标准实验教科书

化学

选修5

有机化学基础

学术顾问

（以姓氏笔画为序）

王　宏　冯智文　李正栓　李丽生　原一川

Academic Advisors

Wang Hong　Feng Zhiwen　Li Zhengshuan

Li Lisheng　Yuan Yichuan

主　编

李昌银

副主编

黄　瑛　彭庆华

General Editor

Li Changyin

Professor of English　Yunnan Normal University

Associate General Editors

Huang Ying

Professor of English　Yunnan Normal University

Peng Qinghua

Professor of English　Yunnan Normal University

云南少数民族经典作品英译文库
Classics of Yunnan Ethnic Groups in English Translation
主编　李昌银　General Editor　Li Changyin
副主编　黄瑛　彭庆华　Associate General Editors　Huang Ying & Peng Qinghua

Chye Hpa Ma and Chye Mi Ma

遮帕麻与遮米麻

演唱◎赵安贤
汉译◎杨叶生
整理◎兰克　杨智辉
英译◎杨慧芳
译校◎[美]包琼

Sung by Zhao Anxian
Translated into Chinese by Yang Yesheng
Edited by Lan Ke & Yang Zhihui
Translated from Chinese into English by Yang Huifang
Revised by Joan Cecile Boulerice

云南出版集团
云南人民出版社

图书在版编目（CIP）数据

遮帕麻与遮米麻：汉、英 / 赵安贤演唱；杨叶生汉译；兰克，杨智辉整理；杨慧芳英译. -- 昆明：云南人民出版社，2020.2

（云南少数民族经典作品英译文库 / 李昌银主编）

ISBN 978-7-222-19070-2

Ⅰ. ①遮… Ⅱ. ①赵… ②杨… ③兰… ④杨… ⑤杨
Ⅲ. ①阿昌族－史诗－中国－汉、英 Ⅳ. ①I222.7

中国版本图书馆CIP数据核字(2020)第028260号

出 品 人 李　维　赵石定
项目统筹 周　祥　殷筱钊
项目组稿 郭木玉
责任编辑 郭木玉　溥　思
装帧设计 马　滨　石　斌
责任校对 明　珍　李凯文　费　珺
责任印制 陆卫华　代隆参

云南少数民族经典作品英译文库
Classics of Yunnan Ethnic Groups in English Translation

遮帕麻与遮米麻
Chye Hpa Ma and Chye Mi Ma

演唱◎赵安贤
汉译◎杨叶生
整理◎兰克　杨智辉
英译◎杨慧芳
译校◎［美］包琼
Sung by Zhao Anxian
Translated into Chinese by Yang Yesheng
Edited by Lan Ke & Yang Zhihui
Translated from Chinese into English by Yang Huifang
Revised by Joan Cecile Boulerice

出　版　云南出版集团　云南人民出版社
发　行　云南人民出版社
社　址　昆明市环城西路609号
邮　编　650034
网　址　www.ynpph.com.cn
E-mail　ynrms@sina.com
开　本　787mm×1092mm　1/16
印　张　12.5
字　数　171千
版　次　2020年2月第1版第1次印刷
印　刷　云南出版印刷集团有限责任公司　云南新华印刷一厂
书　号　ISBN 978-7-222-19070-2
定　价　65.00元

云南人民出版社
微信公众号

序　一

◎李正栓

民族典籍英译是传播中国文化、文学和文明的重要途径，是中华文化走出去的重要组成部分。文化与文学的传播，是一个国家提高文化软实力的重要方式，在文化交流和文明建设中起着不可或缺的作用，对提高国家对外话语权、构建国家对外话语体系以及对建设世界文学都有积极意义。

中国各少数民族拥有许多优秀的典籍，具有很高的文物价值、文学价值和文化价值。各民族的先人们通过口头流传或用文字记述了他们各具特色的文化。各少数民族几乎都有自己民族的创世史、史诗和神话传说。

中国民族典籍独具特色，不可替代。重视民族典籍的翻译和研究工作，对于挖掘各民族优秀文化，保护各民族文明，增强各民族之间的沟通和了解，进一步向世界其他地区传播各少数民族优秀文化，乃至提高我国文化软实力都有着重要意义。不少少数民族聚居地处于祖国边疆，有的处在“一带一路”建设关键部位，有的处在与周边国家进行各种交流的重要位置。

中国民族典籍是世界多元文化的有机组成部分，与其他文化共同造就了世界文化的绚丽多姿。世界正因为其文化多样性才变得缤纷多彩。我国各民族典籍中包含的文化多样性极大地丰富了世界多元、特色鲜明的文化。人们对多样性形成全新的认识角度和思维方式。多样性开阔了人们的视野，丰富了人们思考问题的角度。挖掘这些典籍中所蕴含的教育价值和文化价值，对世界其他民族都有指导和借鉴意义，并且有助于建设我国的文化自信。

民族典籍本身蕴含的特殊价值对加强民族文化了解、促进中外文化交流具有重大意义。民族典籍英译具有文学翻译和文化传递之功能，有对外宣传作用，还是一种文学外交。因此，民族典籍翻译和研究对于维护祖国统一、促进民族团结、稳定边疆以及增强国内各民族和中外文化之间的交流都起着极为重要的作用。

中华人民共和国成立以后，中央政府一直十分重视民族典籍翻译和研究工作，提供了强有力的政策支持，并采取了一系列有效措施，加快了各少数民族典籍的抢救、整理、翻译和研究的进程。中央政府多次召开西藏工作会议和新疆工作会议。近年来，国际和国内对于多元文化高度关注，少数民族文学典籍的翻译已然成为业内研究的热点。

近年来，民族典籍翻译和研究迅猛发展，势头良好。国家大力支持，发放国家社科基金课题，教育部和国家民委也发放课题，扶持了一大批研究者。很多民族典籍翻译课题得以立项并顺利开展；为数不少的民族典籍被翻译成汉语、英语和其他语言并出版发行；越来越多的业界人士致力于这个满富生机的学术领域。

在中国文化走出去的国家战略下，全国少数民族典籍英译学术研讨会陆续召开，已经召开三次。

云南是中国民族最多的省份。人口在5000人以上的少数民族有25个，其中有15个民族为云南所特有，分别是：白族、哈尼族、傣族、傈僳族、佤族、拉祜族、纳西族、景颇族、布朗族、普米族、阿昌族、基诺族、怒族、德昂族、独龙族。其中除白族人口占全国白族人口总数的84%以上外，其他14个民族95%居住在云南。

云南还是我国跨境民族最多的省份。在云南的25个少数民族中，有16个民族跨境而居，分别是：傣族、壮族、苗族、景颇族、瑶族、哈尼族、德昂族、佤族、拉祜族、彝族、阿昌族、傈僳族、布依族、怒族、布朗族、独龙族。

云南少数民族创造了辉煌的文化。据不完全统计，云南少数民族文字文献古籍蕴藏量达10万余册（卷），口传古籍4万余种。云南省民委少数民族古籍整理出版规划办公室为了挽救和保护这些古籍，计划在5年内编纂出版100卷《云南少数民族古籍珍本集成》。这是一个令人瞩目的庞大计划。将这些古籍中的珍品翻译介绍给世界，不仅能够弘扬云南省丰富多彩的民族文化，而且有助于增进与南亚东南亚国家的理解与交流，为“一带一路”倡议的实施做出贡献。

云南师范大学外国语学院很重视这一领域的工作。在外国语学院领导支持下，李昌银教授带领一个由教授和中青年学者组成的团队对精选出来的17部云南少数民族经典作品进行英译，计划在5年内（“十三五”期间）翻译出版。这是一项十分有意义的宏大工程。

这17部民族典籍，内容全部为各民族的英雄史诗或神话传说，具有很高的历史意义和文学价值。这些作品涉及阿昌族、白族、傣族、德昂族、哈尼族、景颇族、拉祜族、苗族、纳西族、普米族、彝族等11个少数民族。

云南师范大学这支翻译队伍实力强大，主要由一些多年从事翻译教学、研究和实践的教授和副教授组成，他们是李昌银、黄瑛、彭庆华、孙兴文、吴相如、刘德周、杨慧芳、郜菊、陈萍、包琼（Joan Cecile Boulerice）等国内外专家学者。他们在云南翻译界都是风云人物。

在民族典籍英译中，这支队伍异军突起，为我国民族典籍英译壮大了声势，必将为中国民族典籍走向世界而成为世界文学的一部分做出新贡献。

民族典籍翻译与研究事业关乎国家的稳定统一，关乎民族关系的和谐发展，关乎世界多元文化的实现。在中国，民族典籍资源极为丰富，有待进一步挖掘、翻译。因此，民族典籍英译前景光明。同时，我们也应意识到，仍有许多濒临消失的少数民族典籍亟待拯救，民族典籍翻译与研究工作任重而道远。

（李正栓，中国英汉语比较研究会典籍英译专业委员会常务副会长兼秘书长、河北师范大学博士生导师）

Foreword by Li Zhengshuan

The translation of Chinese ethnic classics is an important approach in spreading Chinese culture, literature and civilization. It is a crucial component of Chinese culture going global. The spreading of Chinese culture and literature is a national policy and an important way to improve the cultural soft power of China. It plays an indispensable role in the cultural exchange between China and other countries and the development of world literature.

The ethnic groups in China have countless excellent classics with high anthropological, literary and cultural value. The ancestors of each ethnic group have passed down their distinctive culture orally or in writing. Almost all the ethnic groups have their own story of creation, epics, myths and legends.

Chinese ethnic classics are unique and irreplaceable. It is imperative to attach importance to the translation and research of ethnic classics; to explore the excellent ethnic cultures; to protect the civilization of ethnic groups; to enhance the communication and understanding among ethnic groups; to further spread the outstanding culture of ethnic groups to other parts of the world; and to build the cultural strength of China. Many ethnic groups live in the border areas and thus play an important role in the cultural and economic cooperation between China and its neighbors in the context of the Belt and Road Initiative.

Chinese ethnic classics are an important component of the magnificence and diversity of world culture. It is diversity that makes the world so colorful. The cultural diversity of Chinese ethnic classics has greatly enriched the world's pluralism and its distinctive features. People around the world have formed a new understanding of diversity. This diversity has expanded people's horizon and enriched their way of thinking. Digging out the educational and cultural value in these classics can contribute to the construction of China's self-confidence in culture.

The special value of the ethnic classics itself is of great significance to the strengthening of national culture and intercultural communication between China and foreign countries. The translation of ethnic classics is not just a literary exchange, but also a form of cultural communication. It is diplomacy through literature in that it consolidates the cultural ties between China and other countries.

After the founding of the People's Republic of China, the central government attached great importance to the translation and research of ethnic classics, provided a great deal of policy support, and adopted a series of effective measures to speed up the process of rescuing, collating, translating and studying ethnic classics. The central government has convened several working conferences on Tibet and Xinjiang. In recent years, both China and other countries have paid close attention to multiculture. The translation of ethnic classics has become a hot topic.

In recent years, the translation and research of ethnic classics have progressed rapidly and have shown good prospects. The government strongly supports and grants the research projects of the national social science fund. The Ministry of Education and the State Ethnic Affairs Commission are also issuing research projects and giving funding to a large number of researchers. Many research projects on ethnic classics have been approved and carried out. Many ethnic classics have been translated into Chinese, English and other languages and published. More and more professionals have dedicated themselves to this new sphere of learning.

In this context, the academic conferences on translation of ethnic classics are held one after another all around the country. And up to now three have been held.

Yunnan is the province which has the most ethnic groups in China. Besides the Han people, there are 25 ethnic groups, each with a population of more than 5,000. Among them, 15 ethnic groups are unique to Yunnan, which are the Bai, the Hani, the Dai, the Lisu, the Wa, the Lahu, the Naxi, the Jingpo, the Bulang, the Pumi, the Achang, the Jinuo, the Nu, the De'ang and the Dulong. Among these, 84% of the total number of the Bai people in China and 95% of the other 14 ethnic groups are living in Yunnan.

Yunnan is also the province which has the most cross-border ethnic groups. Of the 25 ethnic groups, 16 live across the border, namely: the Dai, the Zhuang, the Miao, the Jingpo, the Yao, the Hani, the De'ang, the Wa, the Lahu, the Yi, the Achang, the Lisu, the Buyi, the Nu, the Bulang and the Dulong.

The ethnic groups in Yunnan have created splendid cultures. According to statistics, the number of classics of Yunnan ethnic groups is more than 100 thousand volumes and classics in oral tradition are more than 40 thousand. In order to save and protect these ancient books, the Office of Classics Collation and Publishing of Yunnan Ethnic Groups Affairs Commission planned to compile and publish 100 volumes of *A Collection of Yunnan Ethnic Group Rare Books* in five years, which is an ambitious plan. The introduction of the ancient classics via translation can not only promote and develop the colorful ethnic cultures of Yunnan, but also contribute to the understanding and exchange between China and countries in South Asia and Southeast Asia and to the implementation of the Belt and Road Initiative as well.

The School of Foreign Languages and Literature of Yunnan Normal University is paying close attention to this field. With the support of the School and the University,

Professor Li Changyin is leading a group of professors and young scholars to do the project of *Classics of Yunnan Ethnic Groups in English Translation*, which includes 17 ethnic classics selected carefully from Yunnan's bountiful ethnic classics. These books are the heroic epics or myths and legends of each ethnic groups with great historical significance and literary value. They will finish the translation in five years (during the Thirteenth Five-Year Plan). After that, all the works will be published by Yunnan People's Publishing House.

The 17 works cover 11 ethnic groups: the Achang, the Bai, the Dai, the De'ang, the Hani, the Jingpo, the Lahu, the Miao, the Naxi, the Pumi and the Yi. All of these groups except the Miao and the Yi are unique to Yunnan.

The translation team of Yunnan Normal University is full of strength and vitality, composed of professors and associate professors who have been occupied in translation teaching, research, and practice for a long time. They are Li Changyin, Huang Ying, Peng Qinghua, Sun Xingwen, Wu Xiangru, Liu Dezhou, Yang Huifang, Gao Ju, Chen Ping, Joan Boulerice and other experts and scholars who are representative figures in the translation field in Yunnan province.

This team is a new force that has suddenly arisen in terms of translating ethnic classics. It is expanding the momentum of ethnic classics translation in China and has made a new contribution for China's ethnic classics to go global and become a part of world literature.

The translation and research of ethnic classics are related to the development of Chinese culture and the realization of multiculturalism in the world. In China, ethnic classics are extremely rich in resources, which require us to make further exploration and research and translate them into other languages. Therefore, the future of translating ethnic classics is bright. At the same time, we should also realize that there are still many ethnic works which are close to extinction and urgently need to be rescued. We still have a long way to go in the fields of translation and research in ethnic classics.

(Li Zhengshuan, Standing Vice Chairman and Secretary General, Classics Translation Committee of CACSEC, PhD supervisor at Hebei Normal University)

序　二

◎王　宏

好友云南师范大学外国语学院李昌银教授来电嘱托我为“云南少数民族经典作品英译文库”的出版写一序言，并随即发来该文库的背景资料，让我“不着急，慢慢写”。我本人从事中国典籍英译及研究，深知少数民族典籍对外传译的重要性，但又是少数民族典籍翻译的门外汉。因此，我是怀着虚心学习的态度来写此序言的。近年来，在中国文化“走出去”战略工程大背景下，在中央和地方各级政府的大力支持下，我国少数民族典籍的对外传译及研究工作顺利开展，取得了很大的进步。请看以下数据：

2008 年，广西百色学院韩家权教授获批国家社科基金项目《布洛陀史诗》（壮汉英对照）。该项目已顺利结项，并于 2013 年 12 月获得中国民间文艺最高奖“山花奖”。

2012 年，广西百色学院外语系翻译团队翻译的国家级非物质文化遗产《壮族嘹歌》（英文版）由广西师范大学出版社正式出版。

2012 年，东北大学秦皇岛分校吴松林教授主编的《蒙古族系列：江格尔（汉英对照）》（上下册）由吉林大学出版社出版。

2013 年，河北师范大学李正栓教授英译《藏族格言诗》

由长春出版社出版发行。

2013年，云南财经大学崔晓霞教授撰写的《〈阿诗玛〉英译研究》收入由王宏印教授主编、民族出版社出版的“民族典籍翻译研究丛书”。

2014年，东北大学秦皇岛分校吴松林教授撰写的《满族档案文献研究》申请到国家社科后期资助，他英译的《英雄格斯尔可汗》由吉林大学出版社出版。

2014年，中南民族大学张立玉教授主持的“土家族主要典籍英译及研究”获批国家社科基金项目。

2015年，西安外国语大学梁真惠副教授撰写的《〈玛纳斯〉翻译传播研究》收入由王宏印教授主编、民族出版社出版的“民族典籍翻译研究丛书”。

与此同时，第一届和第二届全国少数民族典籍英译学术研讨会分别于2012年和2014年在广西民族大学和大连民族学院举行，参加会议的院校分布之广、与会代表数量之众、提交论文数量之多和涉及研究话题之细，十分可喜。2016年还将在中南民族大学举行第三届全国少数民族典籍英译学术研讨会。

为什么少数民族典籍的对外传译及研究工作在短短几年就受到译界的青睐，取得众多成果？我认为，这在很大程度上归于典籍翻译界乃至翻译界同仁对“中国典籍”的重新思考和认识。中国典籍浩如烟海，卷帙浩繁，举世瞩目，是全人类共同的精神财富。但对于中国典籍的理解，我们以前较多限于汉民族的重要文献和书籍，而对少数民族多有忽略。在讨论中国典籍时，也较多关注古代文学作品。其实，中国典籍指“中国清代末年1911年以前的重要文献和书籍”，这就要求我们从事典籍翻译时，不但要翻译古代文学典籍作品，还要翻译古代哲学、科技、法律、医学、经济、军事、天文、地理等诸多方面的典籍作品，不但要翻译汉民族的典籍作品，也要翻译各少数民族的典籍作品。

民族典籍具有该民族的原型符号的特质，蕴藏着能够“遗传”并不断“再生”的文化基因。民族典籍是中华传统文化的内核，同时还是中华传统文化的符号构成规则。中国是具有56个民族的多民族国家，少数民族典籍是我国少数民族勤劳与智慧的结晶，是中华文明、也是世界文明不可或缺的一部分。少数民族典籍对外传译具有跨文化交流的作用，它不但有助于更多的人了解少数民族的独特文化，而且还有助于保护少数民族文化的独特性、维持少数民族文化多样性、促进各民族团结、提升中华文化软实力等。

中国少数民族典籍涉及宗教、文学、历史、语言、医学、天文历算等领域，内容丰富，版本多样，载体特殊，传承奇特。仅以《中国少数民族古籍总目提要》为例，该书于1997年正式立项，全书总体设计约60卷、110册，目前已出版23个民族卷共20册：纳西族卷、白族卷、东乡族卷·裕固族卷·保安族卷、土族卷·撒拉族卷、锡伯族卷、哈尼族卷、回族卷·铭刻、柯尔克孜族卷、羌族卷、毛南族卷·京族卷、仫佬族卷、达斡尔族卷、土家族卷、鄂温克族卷、鄂伦春族卷、赫哲族卷、苗族卷、侗族卷、黎族卷、朝鲜族卷。该书真实地反映了我国各少数民族古籍赋存的全面情况，充实了中国的历史和文化内容，为后人探索各种文化形式的源流、揭示中国社会文化发展的轨迹提供了极为珍贵的资料，为我国乃至世界各国人文科学研究提供了一套新颖而全面的资料，对于弘扬中华民族传统文化具有深远的历史意义和现实意义。

少数民族典籍的对外传译是一项艰巨的工作，涉及将少数民族语言译成汉语、少数民族语言之间的互译和少数民族语言译成外语（主要是英语）。前两类翻译历史源远流长，最早可追溯到春秋战国时代《越人歌》的翻译，即汉、壮语之间的翻译。少数民族典籍译成外语的时间则要晚一些。据考证，维吾尔族古典长诗《福乐智慧》成书于1069年或1070年，目前尚未发现完整的原稿，只存留下来三个抄本，分别为赫拉特抄本、费尔干纳抄本与埃及抄本，其中费尔干纳抄本于12~13世纪用阿拉伯文纳斯赫体抄写，1914年发现于今中亚乌孜别克斯坦纳曼干城，现存于该共和国科学院东方研究所。这是少数民族典籍译介到国外的最早纪录。少数民族典籍外译在现代有了较快发展。一些少数民族典籍，如藏族的《格萨尔王传》、蒙古族的《江格尔》和柯尔克孜族的《玛纳斯》等英雄史诗，云南彝族的《阿诗玛》、维吾尔族的《艾里甫和赛乃姆》等民间叙事长诗已先后被翻译成英语及其他外国文字，为世人所知。这对传承少数民族经典，推动中外文化交流起到了不可替代的作用。然而，还有大量的中国少数民族典籍等待我们去翻译和研究。

云南省少数民族典籍资源十分丰富。据不完全统计，云南少数民族文字文献古籍蕴藏量达10万余册（卷），口传古籍4万余种。“云南少数民族经典作品英译文库”正是依托云南省丰富的少数民族典籍资源，借助云南师范大学外国语学院强大的翻译师资队伍，在云南人民出版社的有力支持下，首次将云南少数民族经典作品成系列对外译介的大力举措。云南师范大学外国语学院对“云南少数民族经典作品英译文库”十分重视，他们首先邀请省内外少数民族语言文化研究专家对云南民族典籍和民族文化经典作品进行筛选，做到“好中选好，优中选优”，同时调配最强的翻译力量承担文库的翻译任务。我粗略看了该文库的选题，发现选题面广，覆盖范围宽，收入了云南省阿昌族、白族、傣族、纳西族、德昂族、哈尼族、景颇族、拉祜族、苗族、普米族和彝族等民族的典籍作品。云南共有25个少数民族，其中11个少数民族的典籍作品都覆盖到了，不少作品还是首次译成英文。这将彻底改变云南少数民族典籍由于对外译介数量较少，不为世界了解的尴尬局面。

对于云南师范大学外国语学院而言，把少数民族典籍英译作为翻译专业的优势特色进行建设，这将对该院的学科建设起到助推作用。“云南少数民族经典作品英译文库”所产生的翻译成果和研究成果将培养出一批优秀的典籍翻译和研究团队，凸显该院在全国的学术特色和学术影响，同时还能将翻译能力和研究能力转化为教学能力，提高云南师范大学外国语学院翻译专业研究生的培养质量，为社会输送高水平的翻译人才，有力地支撑学院翻译专业学科的建设和发展。我对云南师范大学外国语学院的翻译师资队伍较为熟悉。作为云南省唯一获得省级高校优势特色学科建设项目的外国语学院，该院具有雄厚的翻译师资力量，在云南省各高校中当属第一。多年来，该院翻译与跨文化研究团队一直承担着对外交流与合作的各种口笔译项目及任务。由外国语学院精心挑选和确定的“云南少数民族经典作品英译文库”翻译人员绝大多数都是云南省翻译领域里的知名教授或专家，有国外留学经历，且具有扎实的英汉双语语言功底，曾翻译出版多部译著和翻译作品，并且主持和参与过多项翻译项目的研究。我阅读李昌银教授发来的文库翻译人员名单，发现多名我所熟悉的知名教授、博士也在其中，感到格外放心。

“云南少数民族经典作品英译文库”的出版发行是云南省翻译界的一件大事，也是我国少数民族典籍翻译传来的又一佳音。想当年，我和“大中华文库”总协调人李林老师曾在参加全国典籍英译学术研讨会之余一起找到李昌银教授，敦促李教授向学校和同事呼吁，少数民族典籍翻译及研究是富矿，值得快挖、深挖，能早出成果，出大成果。今天，我们当年的心愿变成了美好的现实，心里感到特别高兴。再次热烈祝贺“云南少数民族经典作品英译文库”的顺利出版！

（王宏，中国典籍翻译研究会副会长、苏州大学博士生导师）

Foreword by Wang Hong

My friend Professor Li Changyin of Yunnan Normal University asked me to write a few words for the publication of *Classics of Yunnan Ethnic Groups in English Translation*. I am more than delighted to do it. As I have been doing research in English translation of Chinese classics, I know how important this work is. In recent years, substantial progress has been made in translating Chinese ethnic classics into English and introducing them to the world. Let's look at the following accomplishments.

First of all, several projects in the English translation of ethnic classics have received funding from the National Planning Office of Philosophy and Social Science. The first of these projects is *The Epic of Baeuqloxgdoh* (Zhuang-Chinese-English trilingual version), given funding in 2008 and headed by Professor Han Jiaquan of Baise University in Guangxi Zhuang Autonomous Region. In December 2013, this translation won the Shanhua Award, the most prestigious prize for folk literature and art in China. The second project is *A Study of the Manchu Archives*, written by Professor Wu Songlin of Northeastern University at Qinhuangdao and which was given funding in 2014. The third is *English*

Translation and Study of the Major Classics of the Tujia Ethnic Group, headed by Professor Zhang Liyu of the South-Central University for Nationalities, also granted in 2014.

Secondly, several English translations have been published. In 2012, *Liao Songs of Pingguo Zhuang*, has been listed as one of China's national intangible cultural heritages. It was translated by the School of Foreign Languages, Baise University, and published by Guangxi Normal University Press. Also in 2012, *Jangar* (a Chinese-English bilingual edition), edited by Professor Wu Songlin of Northeastern University at Qinhuangdao, was published by Jilin University Press. In 2013, *Tibetan Gnomic Verses Translated into English*, translated by Professor Li Zhengshuan of Hebei Normal University, was published by Changchun Press. And in 2014, *Heroic Geser Khan*, translated by Professor Wu Songlin of Northeastern University at Qinhuangdao, was published by Jilin University Press.

And thirdly, two important monographs have been published by The Ethnic Publishing House in the *Ethnic Classics Translation Research Series* edited by Professor Wang Hongyin of Nankai University. One is *A Study on the English Translation of* Ashima *by Gladys Taylor* (2013), which was the PhD dissertation of Professor Cui Xiaoxia of Yunnan University of Finance and Economics. The other is *Translation and Dissemination of the Oral Epic Manas* (2015) written by Associate Professor Liang Zhenhui of Xi'an International

Studies University.

Meanwhile, it is encouraging to see that the first conferences on English translation of ethnic classics in China have been held in Guangxi Nationalities University and Dalian Nationalities Institute respectively. Participants were both many and enthusiastic. Many papers were presented and a lot of topics discussed. The third conference will be hosted by South Central Nationalities University in 2016.

Why, then, has this field attracted so much attention from translators and scholars alike and accomplished so much in just a few years? The answer, I believe, lies in a rethinking of what constitutes Chinese classics as an indispensable part of human heritage. We used to see Chinese classics as more or less equal to the classics of the Han people, excluding works by other ethnic groups. Moreover, when we talk about Chinese classics, we focus too much on the literary works of ancient times. Yet Chinese classics actually refer to "important works and books before 1911, the year when the Qing dynasty fell, bringing an end to imperial rule". This definition requires us to pay attention not just to literary works, but also writings in other subjects, such as philosophy, science, law, medicine, economics, military affairs, astronomy, and geography, not only Han works, but writings by other ethnic groups as well.

The classical works of a nation are its archetypal symbols, the major carriers of its cultural genes. Chinese classics make up the core of Chinese tradition. The Chinese nation consists of 56 ethnic groups. Ethnic classics are an important part of not only Chinese traditional culture, but also world civilization. The translation of these works into other languages is important in that it helps to promote cross-cultural communications between China and other countries and to protect and preserve the uniqueness and diversity of ethnic cultures by making them accessible to foreign readers.

Chinese ethnic classics cover a variety of areas, such as religion, literature, history, language, medicine, astrology, and calendar, with numerous editions, special media and unique ways of transmission from generation to generation. Take, for example, *An Anthology of Chinese Ethnic Classics*, a colossal project that includes 110 volumes, 20 of which, from 23 ethnic groups, have been published. The anthology reflects the variety and quantity of China's ethnic classics and provides valuable material and resources for studying, understanding and developing Chinese culture and history in a more comprehensive and sustainable way.

The translation of Chinese ethnic classics into foreign languages is a very demanding job, involving rendering from ethnic languages to Chinese, between ethnic languages, and from ethnic languages (often via Chinese) to foreign languages. The first two types of translation can be traced back to the Spring and Autumn Period, when *The Song of the Yue People* was translated from their mother tongue into Chinese. The earliest translation of ethnic classics into a foreign language is *Wisdom of Royal Glory*, a long poem of the Uygurs, which was rendered from the source language into Arabic and is now in the Oriental Institute of Uzbekistan at Namangan. But it was not until modern times that the translation of ethnic classics into foreign languages accelerated. Noticeably, ethnic epics, such as *The Story of Prince Geser* of the Tibetans, *The Story of Jianggeer* of the Mongolians, *Manas* of the Kyrgyz, and narrative poems such as *Ashima* of the Yi people, *Alip and Salam* of the Uygurs, etc., have been published. These translations have contributed to acquainting the world with Chinese ethnic classics, but many remain to be translated.

Yunnan is rich in ethnic classics, boasting more than 100,000 volumes of written classics and over 40,000 pieces of oral literature. Relying on such bountiful resources, as a collective endeavor of the translation team of the School of Foreign Languages and Literature, Yunnan Normal University and with the help of Yunnan People's Publishing House, *Classics of Yunnan Ethnic Groups in English Translation* is the first project to translate Yunnan ethnic classics into English on a large scale. The School adheres to a professional spirit and academic standard in carrying out the project by selecting the most authoritative texts in the source language (Chinese) and recruiting the best translators from its huge faculty. The selection of the works, covering eleven of the twenty-five ethnic groups of the province, indicates expertise and insight. The implementation of the project will change the embarrassing obscurity of Yunnan ethnic classics by making them known to the world, many of them for the first time.

In light of disciplinary development, the project is of great importance, too. Participating in the translation will strengthen the academic foundation of the teachers, enrich their experience and enhance their translation skills and research ability. This in turn will help them become better teachers and thus able to educate students with higher quality. The publication of the books will add greatly to the faculty accomplishments of the School and raise the academic standing of Yunnan Normal University by taking the first step in this direction among the universities of Yunnan province.

This publication project is a great event not only for Yunnan itself, but also for China. Looking back, I remember that Professor Li Changyin, our friend Li Lin, editor of the *Library of Chinese Classics*, and I talked enthusiastically about initiating something like this in Yunnan when we attended a conference on the translation of ethnic classics in Soochow. Lin and I strongly suggested that Professor Li do it as soon as possible. Now I am very pleased to see our talk becoming reality. Again, my congratulations on the publication of *Classics of Yunnan Ethnic Groups in English Translation*!

(Wang Hong, Vice Chairman of Classics Translation Committee of CACSEC, PhD supervisor at Soochow University)

导　言

“云南少数民族经典作品英译文库”旨在将云南少数民族的经典作品翻译介绍给国外对其感兴趣的英文读者大众。随着以古代汉文经典构成的“大中华文库”的出版发行，学界正将注意力转移到民族典籍的翻译上来。民族典籍是指由民族作家创作的反应民族历史和文化的经典作品。广西、贵州、辽宁、新疆、西藏等省区的大学已经捷足先登。我们云南也理应有所作为。云南拥有全国最多的少数民族。全省25个少数民族中，有15个为云南特有民族，即阿昌族、白族、布朗族、傣族、德昂族、独龙族、哈尼族、景颇族、基诺族、拉祜族、傈僳族、纳西族、怒族、普米族、佤族。这些民族的典籍，有的是原作，有的是汉译本，构成了一个巨大的宝库，我们有义务将其介绍给国外的英语读者和学术界。问题是，先译什么？

云南所有的25个少数民族都创造了自己的经典作品，包括史诗、神话、创世故事、民谣、戏曲、山歌和丧歌，以各种形式流传于各地，总数不下10万卷，这还不包括口传文体。经过调查研究，并征求民族学专家的建议后，我们决定重点翻译史诗和神话。史诗和神话叙述的是民族起源故事，最能反映各民族哲学、历史、文化等的概貌、渊源。我们从汗牛充栋的民族史诗与神话中精选了云南阿昌族、白族、傣族、德昂族、哈尼族、景颇族、拉祜族、苗族、纳西族、普米族、彝族等 11 个少数民族的 17 部最具有代表性的经典作品。这些作品全部都是汉语译本，由既会讲母语又精通汉语的双语学者整理、翻译而成。其中有的是在节庆仪式和表演时从口语录制而来。我们没有选择用民族语言写成的文本，首先是因为很难寻找到民族语和英语俱佳的译者；其次是因为一部分典籍的民族语言文本在民间以多种方言形式流传，情节五花八门。汉语文本系专家仔细整理、翻译而成，因而更具权威性。接下来的问题是：如何译？

在我们选定的 17 部作品中，除了《白国因由》为散文体之外，其余全部为民歌韵文体，诗行长度大致相当，行末有松散押韵，无格律。译诗为诗是最起码的要求。我们遵循的原则有如下几点。

一、若原文为诗歌，译文也必须为诗歌。

二、译文尽可能完整地再现原文的思想内容和意象。

三、译文尽可能再现原文的修辞手段。

四、不改变原文每一节诗的行数，除非万不得已。

五、不使用英文的标准格律，因为原文并不是标准的格律体。采用英文的自然节奏，但诗行长短应大体一致。

六、不用韵，除非符合英文表达习惯且不损害原文内容。

我们所追求的，用苏珊·巴斯奈特的话来说就是“异地播种”，而不是直接移栽树木。关于原文的形式特征，尤其是尾韵，能再现时再现，不能再现时果断放弃。

那谁来翻译呢？本文库是云南师范大学外国语学院的集体项目，因此我们的翻译团队由本院十几位同行加上两位在职攻读翻译专业硕士学位的高校教师组成。所有译者都在高校教授翻译课程，从事翻译研究，不仅发表了翻译论文，也出版了译著。

传统上，人们通常是将外语译为母语，而不是将母语译为外语。但是这种情况正在发生改变。现在许多译者都将母语译为外语。根据耐克·帕科恩[①]和斯图亚特·坎贝尔[②]的论证，将母语译入非母语，能够达到相当高的水平。中国的情形为他们的观点提供了新的论据。中国典籍英译在19世纪由英国汉学家理雅各和翟理斯发起，20世纪在亚瑟·伟利、戴维·霍克思、波顿·沃森、约翰·闵福德、宇文所安等英美汉学家的推动下继续发展。值得注意的是，在这一过程中，旅居西方的华人学者迅速加入到了中国典籍英译的行列中。其中最著名的是辜鸿铭和林语堂。他们主动承担这个任务，因为他们认为西方汉学家的母语并非汉语，其译文往往误读汉语原文本，误解中国文化，自己义不容辞，必须为英语读者提供更忠实的英文翻译。自20世纪50年代开始，越来越多的中国大陆译者投身于典籍英译或重译。在杨宪益、许渊冲、汪榕培、王宏印、王宏、李正栓等当代翻译家和翻译理论家的积极倡导和引领下，典籍英译蔚然成风，势头强劲。许渊冲、王宏、李正栓等都在西方出版社出版了英文译著，这表明他们的英文水平达到了国际上的出版标准。

就本文库而言，我们采取了一系列保障译文质量的措施。我们要求译者尽最大努力拿出代表自己最高水平的译文。文

① 挑战公理：译入非母语. 阿姆斯特丹：约翰·本杰明斯出版公司，2005.
② 译入第二语言. 纽约：劳特里奇出版社，2013.

库的主编们对译文进行仔细研读，纠正理解偏差、语法错误以及格式上的问题。在此基础上，我们采取了一个不可或缺的步骤，请长期在我院从事英语教学工作的美国老师包琼（Joan Cecile Boulerice）对每一个译本进行逐字逐句的修改，使之更自然流畅，更符合英文表达习惯。我们尽了最大的努力。如果译文还存在什么问题，皆由我们负责，与包琼老师无关。

在这里，我们对所有给予我们宝贵帮助和支持的专家学者深表谢忱。感谢云南人民出版社的领导为文库成功申报为“十三五”国家重点出版物出版规划项目和国家出版基金项目给予的大力支持。感谢文库责编、东南亚南亚读物编辑部主任郭木玉，她的严谨和敬业令我们动容。感谢云南师范大学为文库提供了出版资金支持，使译者们不被“眼前的苟且”干扰，能够一心一意地追求“诗和远方”。感谢李正栓教授和王宏教授不仅一直鼓励我们前进，而且欣然为文库作序，从全球视野对其意义进行肯定，极大地提振了我们的信心。感谢包琼老师，她的修改保证了译文的流畅性。最后要特别感谢王宏教授和湖南人民出版社的资深编辑李林先生，是他们的建议促成了本文库的构想。

云南师范大学外国语学院

“云南少数民族经典作品英译文库”编委会

General Introduction

This publication project, *Classics of Yunnan Ethnic Groups in English Translation*, aims at introducing Yunnan ethnic classical works to the world by making them available to native speakers of English who might be interested in them. With the publication of the *Library of Chinese Classics*, which consists only of books written by Han authors in classical Chinese, attention now is being turned to the English translation and publication of ethnic classics, books produced by ethnic writers about their history and culture. Universities in provinces such as Guangxi, Guizhou, Liaoning, Xinjiang, and Xizang, have taken the initiative. We in Yunnan must do something, because Yunnan has the largest number of ethnic groups in China. 15 of the 25 ethnic groups in the province, the Achang, the Bai, the Bulang, the Dai, the De'ang, the Dulong, the Hani, the Jingpo, the Jinuo, the Lahu, the Lisu, the Naxi, the Nu, the Pumi, and the Wa, live in no other place but Yunnan. The classics of these people, either in their own language or in Chinese translations, are a great treasure house, which should be accessible to English readers and scholars. But what works should be translated first?

All the 25 ethnic groups in Yunnan have their classics,

epics, mythology, creation stories, folksongs, folk drama, mountain songs, and funeral lament lyrics, most of which exist in different versions in different places. According to one estimation, there are more than 100,000 volumes of them, excluding those in oral form. After a thorough survey and extensive consultations with experts of ethnic studies, we concluded that priority must be given to epics and mythologies, as they reflect an ethnic people's philosophy, history and culture more than anything else by narrating the stories of where and how they think they came from. From many epics and mythologies, we selected 17 of the most authoritative and popular classics representing 11 Yunnan ethnic groups, the Achang, the Bai, the Dai, the De'ang, the Hani, the Jingpo, the Lahu, the Miao, the Naxi, the Pumi, and the Yi. These works are all in Chinese, translated from the original by bilingual scholars whose mother tongue is their own ethnic language and who are fluent and proficient in Chinese. Some were recorded from their oral form at rituals and performances. We did not choose texts written in the ethnic language, not least because it is very hard to find a translator who is skilled in both the ethnic language and English. Moreover, some of the classics in the ethnic language were circulated in various oral forms and fragments. The published Chinese versions have been carefully edited and translated, hence they are more reliable. The next question is: how to translate them?

It happens that all of the 17 works except one are in verse form, with lines more or less the same length and loose rhymes, but no regular meter. A poem must be rendered into a poem; anything less is unacceptable. So here are the general rules we follow when doing the translation.

One. If the original is verse, the translated text must be verse, too.

Two. Reproduce the ideas and the images of the original as completely as possible.

Three. Reproduce the figures of speech of the original as much as possible.

Four. Do not change the number of lines in a stanza unless absolutely necessary.

Five. Do not use standard meters in English, because the Chinese original does not follow any regular meter. Use the natural rhythm of English instead, but most of the lines should look more or less the same length.

Six. Do not use rhyme unless it comes naturally and is faithful to the content of the original.

What we try to do is, to use Susan Bassnett's words, "transplant the seed", not the tree itself. As for the various aspects of form, particularly meter and end rhyme, we reproduce them when it is possible and abandon them when it is necessary.

Who will do the translations? As this is a collective project of the School of Foreign Languages and Literature of Yunnan Normal University, our team consists of a dozen faculty members and two students from our MA translation program who are already teachers in other universities. All the translators have been teaching translation and doing translation research for a long time. They have published not just academic articles on translation, but also translated books from English to Chinese or vice versa.

Traditionally, people translate into their mother tongue, not into a foreign language. But the situation is changing. Many translators today are translating from their mother tongue into a foreign language. The quality can be good, as Nike K. Pokorn and Stuart Campbell prove in *Challenging the Traditional Axioms: Translation into a non-mother tongue* (Amsterdam: John Benjamins Publishing Company, 2005) and *Translation into the Second Language* (New York: Routledge, 2013) respectively. The case of China provides further evidence for their argument. The translation of Chinese classics into English was initiated by James Legge and Herbert Allen Giles in the 19th century and carried on in the 20th century by Arthur Waley, David Hawkes, Burton Watson, John Minford, Stephen Owen and others. It is noticeable that these English and American sinologists were soon joined by Chinese scholars residing in the West, such as Hongming (Tomson) Gu and Lin Yutang, among others. They took up the job because they thought it was their obligation to give English readers more faithful translations than Western sinologists could, who, as their target language is their mother tongue, often misinterpret the original text and misrepresent Chinese culture. Since the 1950s, there has been an increasingly powerful trend for Mainland Chinese translators to render or re-render Chinese classics into foreign languages, English in particular. In our time, this work is gathering momentum, enthusiastically advocated and actively practiced by such well-known translation experts as Yang Xianyi of Beijing Foreign Language Press, Xu Yuanchong of Beijing University, Wang Rongpei of Dalian Foreign Language Institute, Wang Hongyin of Nankai University, Wang Hong of Soochow University, Li Zhengshuan of Hebei Normal University, and many more. These professors are not just translators, but also scholars in translation studies. More importantly, some of them, Xu Yuanchong, Wang Hong and Li Zhengshuan, for example, have had their translations published by Western publishers, which suggests that their English meets the international standard.

In the case of our project, we request that the translators do their best to produce good translations. When they submit them to us, they should represent the highest level that they can attain. Then the general editors appointed by the School read the translated texts and remove inaccurate renderings and grammar mistakes if there are any. On top of that, we've taken an indispensable measure to ensure that our English is readable. We asked Ms. Joan Cecile Boulerice, an American teacher who has been teaching English in our school since 2009, to read every text that we've translated and improve the English by making it more natural and idiomatic. This is the best we can do. Of course any problems that still remain in the translations are ours. They have nothing to do with our American teacher.

As the project is well under way, we would like to thank all those who have helped to make it possible. Ms. Guo Muyu, director of the South and Southeast Asia Editorial Department, Yunnan People's Publishing House, has been most helpful in our cooperation. In addition, she has added importance to the project by turning it into a national publication project. Yunnan Normal University has supported us by paying the publication fees so that the translators won't have to be burdened with the financial responsibilities for this project. Professor Li Zhengshuan and Professor Wang Hong not only have always encouraged us to go on but have also written the forewords for the project, putting it in a global perspective. Ms. Joan Cecile Boulerice's revision has ensured the fluency of the translated texts. Finally, special thanks must be given to Professor Wang Hong, again, and Mr. Li Lin of Hunan People's Press for their suggestion that has helped us conceive the project from the very beginning.

The General Editors
School of Foreign Languages & Literature
Yunnan Normal University, Kunming

遮帕麻与遮米麻

目录

目录

Contents

Contents

遮帕麻与遮米麻

Chye Hpa Ma and Chye Mi Ma

阿昌的子孙啊，
你记不记得阿公阿祖走过的路？
你知不知道我们阿昌的历史？
你晓不晓得造天织地的天公和地母？

晓不得大树的年轮算不得好木匠，
不会数牙口算什么赶马人？
不懂法术就做不了活袍[①]，
晓不得祖宗怎么献家神？

我是一个老倌人[②]，
故事是先辈传下来的；
造天织地的故事像流水一样，
传了千万代才传到我们这里。

静静地听吧，子孙们，
我来为你们歌唱，
让遮帕麻和遮米麻的故事，
像大盈江水一样长流不断。

① 活袍：阿昌族的巫师。
② 老倌人：指年高、智慧、有威望的老人。

Descendants of the Achang people,
Do you still remember the path that our ancestors walked along?
Did you ever know the history of us Achang people?
Have you heard of the father and mother who created the sky and the earth?

A carpenter knowing nothing about tree rings is not a good carpenter.
Is he a qualified horseman that cannot tell the age of a horse by its teeth?
No one can be a huopao[1] without magic powers.
How can you offer sacrifices to your family gods without knowing who they are?

I am an old horseman[2].
The story has been handed down from our ancestors;
The legend of the creation of the sky and the earth is like a long river,
Taking thousands of generations to reach us.

Listen quietly, children!
I will chant for you
The story of Chye Hpa Ma and Chye Mi Ma,
So that it can flow continuously like the Great Yingjiang River.

① Huopao: an Achang priest.
② Old horseman: an aged wise man of high reputation.

第一部分 创世

Book 1 Creation of the World

在太古的时候没有天，
在太古的时候没有地，
整个的世界混沌不分，
不会刮风也不会下雨。

造天的是天公，
天公就是遮帕麻；
织地的就是地母，
地母就是遮米麻。

今天是个好日子，
我给你们讲故事，
先讲遮帕麻造天，
再讲遮米麻织地。

第一折　遮帕麻造天

造天的是遮帕麻，
他没有裤子也没有衣裳，
只有一根神奇的赶山鞭，
系在腰杆上。

In remote antiquity, there was no sky;
In remote antiquity, there was no earth.
The whole world was in chaos.
There was neither wind nor rain.

The father of the sky, who created the sky,
Is named Chye Hpa Ma;
The mother of the earth, who wove the earth,
Is named Chye Mi Ma.

Today is a good day.
I'll tell you the story
First of how Chye Hpa Ma created the sky,
And then of how Chye Mi Ma wove the earth.

Canto 1 Chye Hpa Ma Creating the Sky

The creator of the sky was Chye Hpa Ma.
He wore no clothing,
But only a magic whip,
Which was tied to his waist.

遮帕麻造天的时候，
带领着三十员神将，
跟随着三十名神兵，
三千六百只白鹤飞来帮忙。

三十名神兵挑来银色的沙，
三十员神将担来金色的沙；
三千六百只白鹤列队飞，
衔来圣洁的仙水拌泥巴。

来到天空的正中央，
遮帕麻在手心里捏泥团：
用闪闪的银沙造月亮，
拿灿灿的金沙造太阳。

遮帕麻造的月亮，
像一塘水清汪汪；
遮帕麻造的太阳，
像一塘火亮堂堂。

遮帕麻用右手扯下左乳房，
左乳房变成了太阴山；

When Chy Hpa Ma started to create the sky,
Thirty divine generals went with him,
Thirty divine soldiers followed him,
And thirty-six hundred white cranes flew to help him.

Thirty divine soldiers brought silvery sand.
Thirty divine generals carried golden sand.
Thirty-six hundred white cranes flew in ranks,
Bringing holy water to make mud.

Reaching the middle of the sky,
Chye Hpa Ma kneaded clay balls in his hand,
Creating the moon out of the glistening silvery sand
And making the sun out of the glittering golden sand.

The moon Chye Hpa Ma created
Looked like a pond of clear water;
The sun Chye Hpa Ma made
Appeared to be a pit of flaming fire.

Chye Hpa Ma tore off his left breast with his right hand;
The left breast became the Moon Mountain.

遮帕麻用左手扯下右乳房，
右乳房变成了太阳山。

（天公遮帕麻呵，
舍去了自己的血肉；
今天的男人没有乳房，
就是因了这个缘故。）

遮帕麻用泥巴包住太阳，
太阳还是烫；
三千六百只白鹤衔来仙水，
洒在火辣辣的太阳上。

遮帕麻张开右手的胳膊，
夹起光闪闪的月亮；
遮帕麻伸出左手的胳膊，
夹起火辣辣的太阳。

迈步踩出一条银河，
跳跃留下一道彩虹，
吐气变作大风、白雾，
流汗化作暴雨、山洪。

Chye Hpa Ma tore off his right breast with his left hand;
The right breast became the Sun Mountain.

(Chye Hpa Ma, the father of the sky,
Gave up his own flesh and blood.
For this reason,
Men today have no bulging breasts.)

Chye Hpa Ma covered the sun with mud,
But the sun was still hot;
Thirty-six hundred white cranes brought holy water,
And sprayed it on the burning sun.

Chye Hpa Ma opened his right arm
And grasped the shining moon;
Chye Hpa Ma stretched out his left arm,
And clamped the burning sun.

He took steps and they became a galaxy;
He took leaps and they formed a rainbow.
His exhalation became strong wind and white fog;
His sweat turned into heavy rain and mountain flood.

遮帕麻举起月亮，
放到太阴山上；
遮帕麻举起太阳，
放到太阳山上。

月亮像一池清水，
吐着银光；
太阴山上设下白银宝座，
派勾娄早芒[①]掌管。

太阳像阿昌人的火塘，
散发着温暖；
太阳山上设下黄金宝座，
派毛鹤早芒[②]掌管。

遮帕麻找来一棵梭罗树，
种在太阴山和太阳山中间。
告诉勾娄和毛鹤：
太阴和太阳要绕梭罗树旋转。

遮帕麻在梭罗树下忙碌，

① 勾娄早芒：阿昌族原始宗教信仰的月亮神。
② 毛鹤早芒：阿昌族原始宗教信仰的太阳神。

Chye Hpa Ma lifted up the moon,
And placed it on the Moon Mountain;
Chye Hpa Ma lifted up the sun,
And put it on the Sun Mountain.

The moon was like a pool of clear water,
Giving out silver light;
A silver throne was set up on the Moon Mountain,
And Ko-lo Tsao-mang① was assigned to take charge of it.

The sun was like the fire pit of the Achang people,
Radiating warmth;
A golden throne was set up on the Sun Mountain,
And Mao-hek Tsao-mang② was assigned to take charge of it.

Chye Hpa Ma found a tree named Reevesia pubescens
And planted it between the two mountains.
He told Ko-lo and Mao-hek:
The moon and the sun should revolve around the tree.

Chye Hpa Ma was busy under the tree,

① Ko-lo Tsao-mang: the moon goddess in the primitive religion of the Achang people.
② Mao-hek Tsao-mang: the sun god in the primitive religion of the Achang people.

造出一座星宿山；
山上安了一个大轮子，
派白鹤推着轮子转。

太阴出来是夜晚，
太阳出来是白天。
月亏月圆分月份，
轮转一圈是一年。

遮帕麻挥舞赶山鞭，
甩出火花一串串；
火花飞到云天里，
变成星宿亮闪闪。

遮帕麻造了东边的天，
东边设下琉璃宝座。
派茫鹤早芒[①]住在东边，
让它把东边的天管着。

东边的天呵，
像清水一样清清吉吉[②]；

① 茫鹤早芒：东边的天神。
② 清清吉吉：阿昌族习惯用语，既有清洁明亮之意，更有万古不变的意思。在每节结尾都要咏唱，既像比喻，更似复沓。

And created the Star Mountain;
On the mountain he set up a big wheel,
Which he assigned a white crane to turn.

It would be night when the moon came out;
It would be day when the sun came out.
One moon waxing and waning would make a month.
One full wheel turn would make a year.

Chye Hpa Ma wielded his whip,
And created cascades of sparks;
The sparks flew into the clouds,
And turned into shining stars.

Chye Hpa Ma created the east side of the sky,
Where he set up a glass throne.
Mang-hek Tsao-mang[①] was assigned to live in the east
To take charge of the eastern sky.

The eastern sky was clean and clear[②]
Like clear water;

① Mang-hek Tsao-mang: god of the eastern sky.
② Clean and clear: It's an Achang idiom, meaning clean and bright or permanent and everlasting. It functions as both metaphor and repetition.

东边的天呵，
像泉水一样清澄见底。

遮帕麻造好了南边的天，
南天设下莲花宝座。
派腊各早列[①]住在南方，
让它把南边的天管着。

南边的天呵，
像清水一样清清吉吉；
南边的天呵，
像泉水一样清澄见底。

遮帕麻造好了西边的天，
西边设下玉石宝座。
派孛劭早芒[②]住在西边，
让它把西边的天管着。

西边的天呵，
像清水一样清清吉吉；
西边的天呵，

① 腊各早列：南方的天神。
② 孛劭早芒：西边的天神。

The eastern sky was as clear
As a transparent spring.

Chye Hpa Ma created the southern side of the sky,
Where he set up a lotus throne.
La-ko Tsao-lye① was assigned to live in the south
To take charge of the southern sky.

The southern sky was clean and clear,
Like clear water;
The southern sky was as clear
As a transparent spring.

Chye Hpa Ma created the western side of the sky,
Where he set up a jade throne.
Bo-shao Tsao-mang② was assigned to live in the west
To take charge of the western sky.

The western sky was clean and clear
Like clear water;
The western sky was as clear

① La-ko Tsao-lye: god of the southern sky.

② Bo-shao Tsao-mang: god of the western-sky.

像泉水一样清澄见底。

遮帕麻造好了北边的天，
北边的天设下翡翠宝座。
北边的天空最尊贵，
派毛弥早芒[①]管着。

北边的天呵，
像清水一样清清吉吉；
北边的天呵，
像泉水一样清澄见底。

遮帕麻造好了天的中央，
遮帕麻定下了天的四极；
勾娄、毛鹤管日月，
毛弥、早芒管天地。

遮帕麻造的天，
存在了万万年；
遮帕麻的功绩，
留在阿昌人的心坎。

---

① 毛弥早芒：北边的天神。

As a transparent spring.

Chye Hpa Ma created the northern side of the sky,
Where he set up an emerald throne.
The northern sky was the most prestigious,
And Mao-mi Tsao-mang① was assigned to take charge of it.

The northern sky was clean and clear,
Like clear water;
The northern sky was as clear
As a transparent spring.

Chye Hpa Ma created the center of the sky;
Chye Hpa Ma fixed four poles to hold up the sky.
Ko-lo and Mao-hek took charge of the sun and the moon.
Mao-mi and Tsao-mang took charge of the sky and the earth.

The sky created by Chye Hpa Ma
Has existed for millions and millions of years;
The heroic deeds of Chye Hpa Ma
Have always been cherished in the hearts of the Achang people.

① Mao-mi Tsao-mang: god of the northern sky.

遮帕麻造的日月，
光辉洒满大地；
遮帕麻的名声，
流传了千万个世纪。

第二折　遮米麻织地

世界上有阴就有阳，
世界上有天要有地。
遮帕麻造天的时候，
遮米麻就开始织地。

她摘下喉头当梭子，
她拔下脸毛织大地；
（从此女人没有了胡须，
从此女人没有了喉结。）

遮米麻拔下右腮的毛，
织出了东边的大地。
东边的地像清水一样清清吉吉，
东边的地像泉水一样清澄见底。

遮米麻的右腮流下了鲜血，

The sun and the moon created by Chye Hap Ma
Have been shining all over the earth;
Chye Hpa Ma has had a good reputation
For thousands of centuries.

Canto 2　Chye Mi Ma Weaving the Earth

Where there is Yin, there is Yang;
Where there is a sky, there will be an earth.
When Chye Hpa Ma started to create the sky,
Chye Mi Ma began to weave the earth.

She took out her larynx and used it as a shuttle;
She pulled out her facial hair and wove the earth with it.
(Since then women have had no beard;
Since then women have had no Adam's apple.)

Chye Mi Ma plucked the hair of her right cheek
And wove the eastern part of the earth with it.
The eastern part of the earth was as clean and clear as water;
The eastern part of the earth was as clear as a transparent spring.

Chye Mi Ma's right cheek shed so much blood

淹没了东边的大地；
东边出现了一片汪洋，
化成东海无边无际。

东海波涛连天，
长满虾、鱼、龟、鳖；
东海里设下水晶宝座，
派东海龙王把它管理。

遮米麻拔下左腮的毛，
织出了西边的大地。
西边的地像清水一样清清吉吉，
西边的地像泉水一样清澄见底。

遮米麻的左腮流下了鲜血，
淹没了西边的大地；
西边出现了一片汪洋，
化作西海无边无际。

西海波涛连天，
长满虾、鱼、龟、鳖；
西海里设下珍珠宝座，
派西海龙王把它管理。

That it flooded the eastern part of the earth;
There appeared a small sea in the east,
Which finally turned into the vast East Sea.

The East Sea was choppy,
Full of shrimps, fishes, tortoises and turtles;
A crystal throne was set up in the East Sea,
And the Dragon King of the East Sea was assigned to take charge of it.

Chye Mi Ma plucked the hair of her left cheek
And wove the western part of the earth with it.
The western part of the earth was as clean and clear as water;
The western part of the earth was as clear as a transparent spring.

Chye Mi Ma's left cheek shed so much blood
That it flooded the western part of the earth;
There appeared a small sea in the west,
Which finally turned into the vast West Sea.

The West Sea was choppy,
Full of shrimps, fishes, tortoises and turtles;
A pearl throne was set up in the west Sea,
And the Dragon King of the West Sea was assigned to take charge of it.

遮米麻拔下下颏的毛，
织出了南边的大地。
南边的地像清水一样清清吉吉，
南边的地像泉水一样清澄见底。

遮米麻的下颏流下了鲜血，
淹没了南边的大地；
南边出现了一片汪洋，
化成南海无边无际。

南海波涛连天，
长满虾、鱼、龟、鳖；
南海里设下珊瑚宝座，
派南海龙王把它管理。

遮米麻拔下额头的毛，
织出了北边的大地。
北边的地像清水一样清清吉吉，
北边的地像泉水一样清澄见底。

遮米麻的额头流下了鲜血，
淹没了北边的大地；

Chye Mi Ma plucked the hair of her lower chin
And wove the southern part of the earth with it.
The southern part of the earth was as clean and clear as water;
The southern part of the earth was as clear as a transparent spring.

Chye Mi Ma's lower chin shed so much blood
That it flooded the southern part of the earth;
There appeared a small sea in the south,
Which finally turned into the vast South Sea.

The South Sea was choppy,
Full of shrimps, fishes, tortoises and turtles;
A coral throne was set up in the South Sea,
And the Dragon King of the South Sea was assigned to take charge of it.

Chye Mi Ma plucked the hair of her forehead
And wove the northern part of the earth with it.
The northern part of the earth was as clean and clear as water;
The northern part of the earth was as clear as a transparent spring.

Chye Mi Ma's forehead shed so much blood
That it flooded the northern part of the earth;

北边出现了一片汪洋，
化作北海无边无际。

北海波涛连天，
长满虾、鱼、龟、鳖；
北海里设下玛瑙宝座，
派北海龙王把它管理。

遮米麻织就了大地，
用的是血肉的躯体；
世界有了依托呵，
万物有了生机。

遮米麻织的大地，
存在了万万年，
遮米麻的功绩，
留在阿昌人的心坎。

大地无边无际，
到处流传着遮米麻的名声；
大海深不见底，
怎么比得上遮米麻的恩情！

There appeared a small sea in the north,
Which finally turned into the vast North Sea.

The North Sea was choppy,
Full of shrimps, fishes, tortoises and turtles;
An agate throne was set up in the North Sea,
And the Dragon King of the North Sea was assigned to take charge of it.

Chye Mi Ma had woven the earth
With her own flesh and blood;
The world had its support;
Everything came to life.

The earth woven by Chye Mi Ma
Has existed for millions and millions of years;
The heroic deeds of Chye Mi Ma
Always stay in the hearts of the Achang people.

The earth is boundless,
And Chye Mi Ma is well-known everywhere;
The sea is fathomless, but how can it be compared with
The kindness of Chye Mi Ma?

阿昌子孙啊，
晒谷的时候，
不要忘记了遮帕麻；
喝水的时候，
不要忘记了遮米麻。

第三折　天公地母传人种

有上必有下，
有天要有地；
地支撑着天，
天覆盖着地。

天刚造就，
地刚织完，
天公遮帕麻呵，
来到大地的东方。

天刚造就，
地刚织完，
地母遮米麻呵，
出现在大地的西方。

Descendants of the Achang,
When you dry grain in the sun,
Do not forget Chye Hpa Ma.
When you drink water,
Do not forget Chye Mi Ma.

Canto 3 Multiplication and Reproduction

Where there is a top, there is a bottom.
When there is a sky, there needs to be an earth;
While the earth supports the sky,
The sky covers the earth.

When the sky had just been created
And the earth had just been woven,
Chye Hpa Ma, the father of the sky,
Arrived in the east of the earth.

When the sky had just been created
And the earth had just been woven,
Chye Mi Ma, the mother of the earth,
Appeared in the west of the earth.

天幕高高张开，
大地平平展展；
天像一个大锅盖，
地像一个大托盘。

天也造得好，
地也织得好，
只是天小地大了，
天边罩不住地缘。

遮帕麻拉拉东边的天，
西边的大地裸露了；
遮帕麻拉拉南边的天，
北边的大地裸露了。

拉天拉出滚滚雷，
雷声震天涯；
雷响三百里，
惊动了遮米麻。

遮米麻抽去三根地筋，
大地皱得像阿昌姑娘的绕裙：
凸的地方变成了高山，

The canopy of the sky opened high;
The earth spread level and wide.
The sky was like a large pot-cover;
The earth looked like a big tray.

The sky was well made,
And the earth was well woven.
But the sky was smaller than the earth,
And the sky could not cover the earth's edges.

When Chye Hpa Ma pulled the sky to the east,
The earth became bare and uncovered in the west;
When Chye Hpa Ma pulled the sky to the south,
The earth became bare and uncovered in the north.

Pulling the sky triggered rolling thunder,
And the thunder shook the world.
The thunder spread three hundred miles,
Startling Chye Mi Ma.

Chye Mi Ma stripped away three earth cords,
And the earth was as wrinkled as Achang girls' skirts:
The bumps became great mountains,

凹的地方便是山箐。

大地卷缩了，
就像晒干的虎皮；
大地缩小了，
天幕才罩住了地的四极。

遮米麻抽去地筋三根，
大地顿时颤抖了。
地震扯动了三千里，
惊动了遮帕麻。

震动平息过后，
山山水水变得无比秀丽。
遮帕麻朝四面看看，
美丽的山河多么神奇。

山头开满栀子花，
朵朵白花似雪洒，
花丛中住着百灵鸟，
百灵鸟叫处种山茶。

山腰开满攀枝花，

And hollow places became valleys.

The earth shrank,
Like the dried hide of a tiger;
The earth became smaller, and the canopy of the sky
Could finally cover the four poles of the land.

When Chye Mi Ma stripped away the three cords,
The earth trembled.
The earthquake moved three thousand miles,
Which shocked Chye Hpa Ma.

After the earthquake had died down,
The mountains and waters became incomparably beautiful.
Chye Hpa Ma looked around,
Amazed by the beautiful mountains and rivers.

Gardenia flowers bloomed over the top of the mountains,
And the white flowers looked just like snow.
Among the flowers lived larks.
Where the larks sang, there grew camellia trees.

The mountainsides were covered with kapok flowers,

枝枝花开像火把，
花树上住着白鹇鸟，
白鹇欢鸣好安家。

山脚绣泵[1]遍地黄，
花中住着金凤凰；
绣泵花开等蜂采，
凤凰合鸣寻伙伴。

“是什么样的巧手把大地织就？
是什么样的巧手把大地打扮？”
遮帕麻要寻找地母，
把千山万水走遍。

天罩住了大地，
好像盖房子有了屋顶；
五光十色的天空，
使遮米麻高兴万分。

天上星星数不清，
月亮落山太阳升。
太阳落下天就黑，

① 绣泵：花名，一种黄色的花。

And the branches full of kapok flowers looked like torches.
On the flower trees lived silver pheasants,
Which settled down and sang happily.

The foot of the mountains was all yellow with xiubeng[①],
And among the flowers lived golden phoenixes.
The flowers were blooming for bees to gather their nectar,
And phoenixes sang in chorus to attract their partners.

"What deft hands have woven the earth?
What skillful hands have adorned it? "
Chye Hpa Ma went over all mountains and rivers
In order to find the mother of the earth.

The sky covered the earth
In the way a roof covered a house.
The sky in all its colors
Gave Chye Mi Ma her greatest joy.

There were countless stars in the sky.
The moon set and the sun rose.
When the sun set, it became dark.

① Xiubeng: a kind of yellow flowers.

太阳升起天就明。

“是谁拉开的天幕？
是谁安排的四极？”
没有太阳，月亮不发光；
不见天公，难解遮米麻心头的谜。

遮帕麻寻地母，
下深箐、上高山，
深箐喝泉水，
高山找食粮。

野味生肉充饥，
嫩叶竹笋作粮，
石洞深处藏身，
光滑石板作床。

剥下树皮当盖头[①]，
连起兽皮作衣裳。
藤子腰间系，
打着光脚板。

① 盖头：古时候搭在头顶遮避日光、风雨的用具。

When the sun rose, it was dawn.

"Who opened the canopy of the sky?
Who arranged the four poles?"
Without the sun, the moon would not shine;
Only the father of the sky could solve Chye Mi Ma's puzzles.

In order to find the mother of the earth,
Chye Hpa Ma went through deep valleys and high mountains,
Drinking water in deep valleys,
And seeking food in high mountains.

He ate wild fruit and raw meat to satisfy his hunger
And took tender leaves and bamboo shoots as food;
He sheltered in deep caves,
Using smooth pieces of slate as his bed.

He shaved off bark as a head cover①,
Made clothes out of animal skins,
And fastened rattan around his waist.
But he wore nothing on his feet.

① Head cover: It was used to shelter the head from sun and rain in ancient times.

一个美好的日子，
遮帕麻来到了大地的中央。
潺潺的流水清悠悠，
凉凉的泉水亮汪汪。

遮米麻找天公，
下深箐、上高山，
深箐喝泉水，
高山找食粮。

山果野梨充饥，
鲜花雀蛋作粮，
树洞里面藏身，
大树枝丫当床。

折叠芭华[①]当盖头，
编起石华[②]作衣裳。
藤子腰间系，
打着光脚板。

一个美好的日子，

①芭华：阿昌语，即芭蕉叶。
②石华：阿昌语，即树叶。

On a good day,
Chye Hpa Ma came to the center of the earth,
Where clear water was babbling,
And the cool spring water was bright and clean.

In order to find the father of the sky,
Chye Mi Ma went through deep valleys and high mountains,
Drinking water in deep valleys,
And seeking food in high mountains.

She ate wild fruit to satisfy her hunger,
And took flowers and bird eggs as food;
She sheltered in deep tree hollows,
And used tree branches as her bed.

She folded bahua leaves[①] as a head cover,
Wove clothes out of shihua[②] tree leaves,
And fastened rattan around her waist.
But she wore nothing on her feet.

On a good day,

① Bahua leaves: banana leaves in the Achang language.
② Shihua: tree leaves in the Achang language.

遮米麻来到了大地中央。
潺潺的流水清悠悠，
凉凉的泉水亮汪汪。

遮帕麻来了，
流水伴他把俄罗①唱；
遮米麻来了，
泉水映出她美丽的模样。

唱一曲欢乐的“巴松昆②”，
遮帕麻的笑脸像天空一样晴朗；
唱一曲热烈的“巴套昆③”，
遮米麻的眼睛像月亮那样明亮。

小鸟在树上唱歌，
天公地母在树下相逢，
好听的话啊，
像山泉淙淙。

遮米麻说：“你造的天真好。
没有你造的月亮，

---

① 俄罗：阿昌族古老调子，传说遮帕麻从天上带来。
② 巴松昆：阿昌族古老的民歌曲调。
③ 巴套昆：阿昌族古老的民歌曲调。

Chye Mi Ma came to the center of the earth,
Where clear water was babbling,
And the cool spring water was bright and clean.

There came Chye Hpa Ma,
Who, accompanied by running water, sang to the eluo[1] tune.
Here came Chye Mi Ma,
Whose beauty was reflected in the water.

After singing a melodious Ba-sok Hkun[2] song,
Chye Hpa Ma's smiling face was as clear as the sky;
After singing an exciting Ba-htao Hkun[3] song,
Chye Mi Ma's eyes were as bright as the moon.

Birds were singing in the trees,
While the father of the sky and the mother of the earth met under the tree;
Sweet words were uttered
Like the gurgling of a spring.

Chye Mi Ma said, "You have made a perfect sky.
Without the moon you have made,

① Eluo: It is one of Achang music tunes said to come from heaven.
② Ba-sok Hkun: It is one of the Achang people's ancient folk music tunes.
③ Ba-htao Hkun: It is one of the Achang people's ancient folk music tunes.

夜里看不见道路，
就连夜莺也不敢歌唱。

“没有你造的太阳，
万物不会生长；
没有你造的天，
我织的大地一片黑暗。”

遮帕麻说：“我造的天再好，
比不上你织的大地；
没有大地的支撑，
天空就会像云彩随风飘移。

“大地有巍峨的高山，
大地有辽阔的平原，
大地有肥美的坝子，
大地有宽阔的海洋。”

遮米麻说：“山高没有打猎人，
林深没有砍柴人，
地阔没有种田人，
海宽没有捕鱼人。”

We can't see the road at night,
And even nightingales dare not sing.

"Without the sun you have made,
Nothing would grow;
Without the sky you have made,
The earth I have woven would be all dark."

Chye Hpa Ma said, "The sky I have made may be good,
But it is not as good as the earth you have woven.
Without the support of the earth,
The sky would be drifting in the wind as clouds do.

"The earth has high mountains.
The earth has vast plains;
The earth has its fertile flatlands;
The earth has vast oceans."

Chye Mi Ma said, "There are no hunters on the high mountains.
There are no woodcutters in the deep forests.
There are no farmers on the vast plains.
There are no fishermen on the vast oceans."

遮帕麻说："世上有了造天的人，
世上有了织地的人；
天和地已经合拢，
我们为什么还不合在一起？

"让我们同在一眼井里打水，
让我们同在一座山上狩猎，
让我们同围一个火塘吃饭，
让我们同在一个窝里安身。"

遮米麻说："这要去问你的爹，
这要去问你的妈；
你爹同意才能成亲，
你妈同意才能成家。"

遮帕麻说："我没有爹，
我也没有妈，
要问就去问天吧，
看天意许不许我们成一家？"

遮帕麻指着磨盘说：
"我从东山滚磨盖，
你从西山滚磨底，

Chye Hpa Ma said, "Here is the maker of the sky,
And here is the mother of the earth.
The sky and the earth have been connected.
Why aren't we connected?

"Let's draw water from the same well,
Let's hunt on the same mountain,
Let's eat together around a fireplace,
Let's rest in the same den."

Chye Mi Ma said, "You should talk to your father about this,
And you should talk about this with your mother.
We cannot get married without your father's agreement,
And we cannot get married without your mother's approval.

Chye Hpa Ma said, "I have no father,
And I don't have a mother either.
If we need to ask someone, shall we ask the sky
And see whether its plan is for us to be a family?"

Chye Hpa Ma pointed to the millstone and said:
"I will roll the runner stone from the east mountain,
And you roll the bedstone from the west mountain.

磨盖磨底合拢就成婚。”

遮米麻指着两座山说：
“我在北山烧柴火，
你在南山烧柴火，
两山火烟相交我们就结合。”

遮帕麻上东山，
遮米麻上西山，
东山滚下磨盖，
西山滚下磨底。

西山磨底滚到山脚，
东山磨盖滚到山底，
磨盖磨底心对心，
紧紧合在一起。

遮帕麻上南山，
遮米麻上北山，
两山同时点柴火，
两山同时冒火烟。

南山火烟向北，

We will get married if the two can meet for closure."

Chye Mi Ma pointed to two mountains and said:
"I burn firewood in the north mountain,
And you burn firewood in the south mountain.
We will unite as a family if the smoke from the two mountains meet."

Chye Hpa Ma went to the east mountain,
While Chye Mi Ma went to the west mountain.
Down the east mountain rolled the runner stone,
And down the west mountain rolled the bedstone.

The bedstone stopped at the foot of the west mountain,
And the runner stone rolled to the bottom of the east mountain.
The runner stone and the bedstone met well
And reached closure perfectly.

Chye Hpa Ma went to the south mountain,
And Chye Mi Ma went to the north mountain.
Firewood was simultaneously lit on the two mountains,
And the two fires gave out smoke at the same time.

The smoke from the south mountain floated northward,

北山火烟向南，
两山火烟相交，
合成一股青烟在高空盘旋。

山头火烟相交，
山底磨盘相合，
遮帕麻和遮米麻，
从此做了一家。

结婚九年才怀胎，
怀胎九年才临产；
生下一颗葫芦籽，
把它种在大门旁。

九年葫芦才发芽，
发芽九年才开花，
开花九年才结果，
结了一个葫芦有磨盘大。

遮帕麻走到葫芦下，
葫芦里面闹喳喳。
剖开葫芦看一看，

While the smoke from the north mountain floated southward.
The two chains of smoke met
To form blue smoke spiraling high in the air.

The fire smoke met over the mountains,
And the two parts of the millstone met at the foot of the mountains.
Chye Hpa Ma and Chye Mi Ma
Thus became one family.

After nine years of marriage
And another nine years of pregnancy,
They finally bore a gourd seed,
Which they planted by the gate.

It took nine years for the gourd seed to sprout.
It took nine years for the sprout to bloom.
It took nine years before the flower bore fruit,
Which was as big as a millstone.

Chye Hpa Ma went up to the gourd
And heard twittering inside.
He opened the gourd

跳出九[1]个小娃娃。

老大跳出来，
看见园里开桃花，
以“陶”（桃）为姓是汉族，
住到平坝种庄稼。

老二跳出来，
看见长刀挂在葫芦架，
以“刀”为姓是傣族，
住在河边捕鱼虾。

老三跳出来，
看见李树开白花，
以“李”为姓是白族，
洱海边上去安家。

老四跳出来，
听见门前河水响哗哗，
以“和”（河）为姓是纳西，
丽江坝子去养马。

① 九：不是实数，泛指多数。

And saw nine[1] little babies jumping out of it.

The first baby jumped out
And saw peach flowers in the garden.
"Tao" (meaning "peach") was thus the surname for the Han people,
Who went to live in the plain areas and planted crops.

The second baby jumped out
And saw a long knife hanging on the gourd shelf.
"Dao (meaning "knife") was thus the surname for the Dai people,
Who went to live by the river and caught fish and shrimps.

The third baby jumped out
And saw the plum trees with white flowers.
"Li " (meaning "plump") was thus the surname for the Bai people,
Who went to settle down by Erhai Lake.

The fourth baby jumped out
And saw the gurgling river in front of the house.
"He" (meaning "river") was thus the surname for the Naxi people,
Who went to Lijiang and raised horses on the Lijiang plain.

① Nine: In this context it does not refer to the exact number nine but means a very big number.

老五跳出来，
看见牛打架，
以“牛”为姓是哈尼，
向阳山坡去种茶。

老六跳出来，
看见竹箩靠墙下，
以“罗”（箩）为姓是彝族，
彝族力大背盐巴。

老七跳出来，
看见石板光又滑，
以“石”为姓是景颇，
打把长刀肩上挎。

老八跳出来，
看见杨柳吐新芽，
以“杨”为姓是崩龙[1]，
崩龙纺线弹棉花。

老九是个小姑娘，

① 崩龙：德昂族的旧称。

The fifth baby jumped out
And saw bulls fighting.
"Niu" (meaning "bull") was thus the surname for the Hani people,
Who planted tea on the sunny hillsides.

The sixth baby jumped out
And saw a bamboo basket against the wall.
"Luo" (meaning "bamboo basket") was thus the surname for the Yi people,
Who had strong backs and went to carry salt.

The seventh baby jumped out
And saw the smooth slate.
"Shi" (meaning "slate") was thus the surname for the Jingpo people,
Who forged a long knife and slung it over the shoulder.

The eighth baby jumped out
And saw willows budding.
"Yang" (meaning "willow") was thus the surname for the Benglong[1] people,
Who spun yarn and fluffed cotton.

The ninth baby was a little girl,

① Benglong: an old name for the De'ang people.

遮米麻最喜欢她，
留在身边学织布，
织出腰带[①]似彩霞。

老九很勤快，
天天起得早，
以“早”为姓是阿昌，
阿昌住在半山腰。

九种民族同是一个爹，
九种民族同是一个妈，
九种民族子孙多得像星星，
九种民族原本是一家。

① 腰带：阿昌族姑娘最讲究腰带，小伙子们常以姑娘织的腰带来识别她们是否能干。

Whom Chye Mi Ma loved best.
She stayed around and learned to weave.
The girdles[1] she knitted were as beautiful as rosy clouds.

She was diligent
And got up early every day.
Thus "Zao" (meaning "early") was the surname for the Achang people,
Who lived halfway up the mountains.

The nine ethnic groups share the same father;
The nine ethnic groups share the same mother.
The nine ethnic groups have numerous descendants like countless stars,
But the nine ethnic groups were originally from the same family.

① Girdle: Achang girls pay particular attention to exquisite artistry of their waist belts because Achang men usually identify a girl's capability according to the belts she knits.

第二部分　补天治水

Book 2　Mending the Sky, Controlling Water

自古有阴就有阳，
自古有恶也有善，
有福便有祸，
祸福常相伴。

没有雨水鲜花不会开放，
雨水多了江河又会泛滥。
雨水给阿昌带来过幸福，
雨水也给阿昌制造过灾难。

阿昌的子孙啊，
要是窝铺漏雨，
不要责怪雨水，
赶快把房顶修理。

第一折　遮米麻补天

阿昌、景颇住山寨，
山上有了砍柴打猎人；
汉族、傣族住平坝，
坝子有了种田打鱼人。

绿绿的庄稼长得好，

Ever since the ancient times, there has been Yin and Yang;
Ever since time immemorial, there have been good and evil.
Woe goes to those who are blessed;
Misfortune and fortune often go hand in hand.

Flowers will not bloom without rain;
Rivers overflow when there is too much rain.
Rain has brought happiness to the Achang;
Rain has also caused disaster for the Achang.

Descendants of the Achang,
If your huts leak,
Don't blame the rain,
But repair the roof quickly.

Canto 1　Chye Mi Ma Mending the Sky

As the Achang and the Jingpo people lived in mountain villages,
There were woodmen and hunters in the mountains;
As the Han and the Dai people lived on the plains,
There were farmers and fishermen in the plains.

Green crops grew well.

肥壮的牛羊跑满山。
风调雨顺的好日子呵，
过了七七四十九年。

不知哪年哪月的一个早晨，
东方的太阳还没有升起，
寨子里的人们还在安睡，
灾难忽然降临。

地下掀起狂风，
天上堆满黑云，
阳春三月下暴雨，
四十九天还不停。

高山被摧崩，
深谷被填满，
树林被扫平，
日月失去了光芒。

春天的雷雨，
把窝里的小鸟打落；
铺天盖地的洪水，
淹没了山寨村落。

Fat cattle and sheep ran all over the mountains.
Wind and rain came at the right time,
And good days lasted for forty-nine years.

On a morning not quite certain to remember,
The sun in the east had not yet risen.
While people in the village were still sleeping,
Disaster struck all of a sudden.

The wind was blowing over the earth.
The sky was covered with dark clouds.
Heavy rain poured down in sunny March,
And it went on and on for forty-nine days.

High mountains were destroyed.
Deep valleys were filled to the full.
Trees were swept away.
The sun and the moon lost their light.

Thunderstorms in spring
Knocked the birds out of their nests;
Blanketing floods
Drowned the mountain villages.

大地变成了一片汪洋，
山峰像一只飘荡的小船；
白天看不见太阳，
晚上看不见月亮。

不是遮帕麻造小了天，
也不是遮米麻抽地线，
是天地没有合拢，
狂风卷起了天的四边。

天破了地母会补，
她早已把三根地筋绕成了线团；
三根地筋用来补天，
缝合了天地的三个边缘。

第一根地筋缝合了东边的天地，
太阳和月亮从那儿升起。
东边不再刮大风，
东边不再下暴雨。

第二根地筋缝合了西边的天地，
太阳和月亮到那儿歇息。

The earth became a sea.
The mountain was like a floating boat;
The sun was out of sight during the day,
And the moon was not visible at night.

It was not that Chye Hpa Ma made the sky too small;
It was not that Chye Mi Ma stripped away some cords of the earth.
It was that the sky did not fit the earth properly,
And the strong wind had whipped up the four edges of the sky.

The mother of the earth would mend it when the sky was broken.
She had already wound the three cords of the earth into a reel of thread;
Now they were used to mend the sky,
And three edges of the sky and the earth were stitched together.

The first cord stitched up the sky and the earth in the east.
The sun and moon rose again from there.
There was no more strong wind in the east,
And there were no more torrential rains there either.

The second cord stitched up the sky and the earth in the west.
The sun and moon went there again to rest.

西边不再刮大风，
西边不再下暴雨。

第三根地筋缝合了北边的天地，
北斗高挂笑眯眯。
北边不再刮冷风，
北边不再下暴雨。

缝好东、西、北三边天地，
三根地筋已经用尽。
南边的天地无线补，
南边的暴雨还在下个不停。

第二折　遮帕麻造南天门

要补南边的天，
要救南方的难，
天公告别地母，
去到南方拉涅旦[1]。

高山挡住去路，
遮帕麻挥动赶山鞭，

① 拉涅旦：传说中的南极。

There was no more strong wind in the west,
And there were no more torrential rains there either.

The third cord stitched up the sky and the earth in the north,
The Big Dipper again hung high happily.
There was no more cold wind in the north,
And there were no more torrential rains there either.

Stitching the east, west and north sides of the sky and the earth,
The three cords had been used up.
There was no cord for stitching the south side;
Heavy rain was still falling in the south.

Canto 2　Chye Hpa Ma Building the South Sky Gate

In order to mend the southern sky,
And in order to save the south from disaster,
The father of the sky bid farewell to his wife, the mother of the earth,
And went to La-nye Tan①.

When high mountains stood in the way,
Chye Hpa Ma wielded his whip.

① La-nye Tan: the Antarctic Pole in this legend.

群山像驯服的牛羊，
听从遮帕麻驱赶。

河水挡住去路，
遮帕麻横放赶山鞭，
鞭子变成一座桥，
跨到了河的对岸。

遮帕麻来到拉涅旦，
这里还是一片汪洋。
没有地线缝补南天，
只好筑一道遮风挡雨的墙。

筑墙要用九拿[①]长的石头，
修门要用九丈宽的木板；
找石头要到九十九里外，
找木板九十九天才回转。

神兵抬石脚打颤，
神将解板汗如雨。
做重活呵太劳倦，
一个个浑身无力摇摇晃晃。

---

① 拿：古时民间衡量长度的方法，一拿约5市尺。

The mountains acted like tame flocks and herds,
And yielded to Chye Hpa Ma's whip.

When rivers blocked the road,
Chye Hpa Ma straightened his whip.
The whip turned into a bridge,
Which connected the two banks of the river.

Chye Hpa Ma came to La-nye Tan,
And it was a broad sea.
There being no cord to stitch the southern sky,
He had to build a wall to keep out the wind and rain.

A nine-arm-span[①] stone would be needed to build the wall;
A nine-zhang-wide plank would be needed to build the gate.
He had to walk ninety-nine miles to get the stone;
He needed ninety-nine days to find the plank.

Divine soldiers shivered as they lifted the stone.
Divine generals were soaked with sweat as they sawed the plank.
Tired from doing such heavy work,
They were all exhausted and shaky.

① Arm span is a unit of measurement equalling about 1.67 metres.

拉涅旦有个智慧的盐婆，
名字叫作桑姑尼[1]。
她炒菜放盐巴，
将士吃了才又有了力气。

木板做框石垒墙，
筑起南天门来挡风雨。
南方不再刮大风，
南天不再下暴雨。

拉涅旦的天空又出现了彩霞，
拉涅旦的大地又种上了庄稼。
风刮断了的大树重发新枝，
水泡烂了的藤子又吐新芽。

枯树发芽靠春风，
拉涅旦离不开恩人遮帕麻；
青藤喜缠大青树，
桑姑尼爱上了英雄遮帕麻。

① 桑姑尼：传说中聪明美丽的女人。阿昌人至今仍用她来比喻贤惠能干的妇女。

In La-nye Tan there lived a wise salt lady,
Whose name was Sang-gu Ni[1].
She added salt when cooking dishes,
And that helped the soldiers regain their strength.

With the plank as the frame and the stone as the wall,
The south sky gate was built to keep out the rain.
There was no more strong wind in the south;
There was no more heavy rain in the south.

In the sky over La-nye Tan rosy clouds appeared again.
The land in La-nye Tan was planted with crops again.
The huge trees broken by wind re-budded;
The listless vines, rotten from rain, sprouted new buds.

Dead trees sprouted in the spring wind;
La-nye Tan would not have survived without its benefactor Chye Hpa Ma;
Green vines preferred to entwine big green trees;
Sang-gu Ni fell in love with the hero Chye Hpa Ma.

---

① Sang-gu Ni: She was said to be a clever and beautiful woman and today she is still a symbol of a kind and capable woman in Achang culture.

第三部分　妖魔乱世

Book 3　The Demon Ruining the World

阿昌的子孙呵，
风不刮树树不弯；
水蛇不撵鱼，
池潭不会起波浪。

豹子出了窝，
黄麂子就要满山逃窜；
世上有了妖魔，
百姓就要遭受苦难。

正当鲜花开得最香，
正当稻谷熟得最黄，
正当牛羊长得最壮，
大地中央却出了个乱世魔王。

第一折　腊訇作乱

世界像一只手掌，
故事发生在手掌的中央。
遮米麻在家织布，
遮帕麻还在南方。

妖精腊訇出世了，

Descendants of the Achang,
Trees do not bend if the wind does not blow.
If water snakes do not catch fish,
The pool will not swell with waves.

If a leopard walks out of its lair,
Deer will flee across the mountains.
If there are demons in the world,
People on the earth will suffer.

While flowers were blooming most sweetly,
While the rice was the most yellow,
While sheep and cattle grew their strongest,
There appeared on the earth a demon to cause troubles.

Canto 1　La Hong Staging an Insurrection

The world is like the palm of a hand.
The story took place in the middle.
Chye Mi Ma was weaving at home;
Chye Hpa Ma was still in the south.

Now there appeared on the earth the demon La Hong,

他是一个凶狠的魔王，
但不知他生在哪里，
也不知他来自何方。

腊訇有兵有将，
心毒手辣像恶狼，
刚刚来到大地中央，
便想独霸这块地方。

他翻着眼睛看太阳，
心里在恶毒地盘算，
“遮帕麻造的太阳，
升起还要降。

“世上发光发亮的东西，
都是热乎乎的一团，
遮帕麻造的月亮，
有光无热空挂天上。

“我要造一个不会落的太阳，
让世界只有白天没有夜晚，
让人们不分昼夜做活路，
让我的名声永远传扬。”

Who was a vicious devil.
No one knew where he was born.
Neither did anyone know where he came from.

La Hong owned some generals and soldiers,
And he was callous and cruel like a heartless wolf.
No sooner had he come into the middle of the earth,
Than he wanted to dominate the place.

He rolled his eyes and looked up at the sun,
With a wicked calculation in mind:
"The sun made by Chye Hpa Ma
Rises and falls.

"The things that shine in the world
All give off heat;
But the moon made by Chye Hpa Ma
Gives out light without heat, hanging useless in the sky.

"I will make a sun that will never set,
So that there is no night but only day in the world,
So that people can work day and night.
And then my fame will spread far and wide.

腊訇使尽牛力气，
射上去一个假太阳，
牢牢钉在天幕上，
不会升也不会降。

遮米麻在家织布纺线，
手也麻了，脚也酸了，
织出的布已有九丈长，
怎么天空还是亮堂堂？

走出门来看一看，
太阳高高挂天上。
不知它何时才落山呀，
心里好生奇怪。

她等着太阳落，
可是等了三年还不降。
天空好像燃烈火，
地面比烧红的锅还烫。

水塘烤干了，
树林晒枯了，

La Hong exhausted all his strength
And finally succeeded in shooting up a fake sun,
Which was nailed to the canopy,
Neither rising nor falling.

Chye Mi Ma was spinning yarn and weaving cloth at home.
She worked until her hands were numb and her feet felt sore.
The cloth she had woven was already as long as nine zhang,
But why was the sky still bright?

She went out to have a look
And saw the sun still hanging high in the sky.
She could not help wondering
When on earth the sun would set.

She waited for the sun to set.
But after three years of waiting, it never set.
The sky was like a blazing fire;
The ground was hotter than a hot pan.

Ponds went dry.
The woods withered.

土地开裂了，
再没有地方躲阴凉了。

水牛的角晒弯了，
从此水牛的角是弯的了；
黄牛的皮烤黄了，
从此黄牛的皮是黄的了。

野猪的背脊烧糊了，
从此野猪脊背是黑的了；
猫头鹰被晒怕了，
从此猫头鹰在白天闭着眼睛了。

鸭子把嗓子哭哑了，
从此鸭子是哑嗓；
飞蝉把肠子气断了，
从此飞蝉没有了肚肠。

腊訇颠倒了阴阳，
整个世界一片混乱：
山族动物被赶下水，
水族动物被赶上山。

The ground cracked.
There was no place for shade.

The buffalo's horns were bent from too much heat;
Ever since then the buffalo's horns have been bent.
The skin of the ox turned yellow because of the heat.
Ever since then the ox's skin has been yellow.

The back of the boar was burnt;
Ever since then the back of boars are black.
Owls were afraid of the hot sun;
Ever since then owls close their eyes during the day.

The duck cried itself hoarse;
Ever since then ducks have a hoarse voice.
The flying cicada got so angry that its intestines were broken;
Ever since then, flying cicadas have no intestines.

La Hong reversed Yin and Yang;
The world was in chaos:
Mountain animals were forced to enter the water.
The aquatic animals were driven up to the mountains.

树木倒着生，
竹根朝天长，
游鱼在山头打滚，
走兽在水里漂荡。

一条大鱼滚到山凹里，
硬着头皮朝土里钻，
鱼鳞烤硬变甲壳，
鱼头烤焦了缩成一团。

这条大鱼变成了穿山甲，
打个山洞躲太阳，
钻在里边不露影，
捕捉蚂蚁作食粮。

蛇毒毒不过七步青[①]，
心狠狠不过腊訇精。
世界沉入火海里，
腊訇更加得意忘形：

“遮帕麻造的天再大，

① 七步青：一种形体短小的毒蛇，据说人被它咬后，走不出七步就会死。

Trees grew upside down;
Bamboo roots grew into the air.
Fish rolled on the top of the mountains;
Terrestrial animals floated in the water.

A big fish carelessly rolled into a hollow
And had to drill hard into the earth:
Its scales hardened into crusts;
Its head was burnt and shrunk into a ball.

This big fish became a pangolin.
It dug a cave to hide itself from the sun.
It hid in the shadow and would not come out.
It hunted ants for food.

No snake was more poisonous than the seven-step green snake[①].
No man was as merciless as the demon La Hong.
The world had sunk into flames,
And La Hong became even more complacent.

"No matter how great the sky that Chye Hpa Ma created,

① Seven-step green snake: It is a small snake that is so poisonous that the victim dies before he can walk seven steps.

没有我的神通大；
遮米麻织的地再宽，
不够我把魔法施展。

“天上地下我都要管，
强者就要做大王。
谁敢阻挡我，
叫他活不长。

“杀谁留谁全在我，
不管别人怎么说；
东西南北我安排，
生生死死我掌握。”

被恶狼冲散的羊群，
会“咩咩”地把主人叫唤；
被狂风吹散的小鸟，
会“啾啾”地寻找伙伴。

看到生灵遭到灾难，
遮米麻心急似油煎。
无力制服腊訇啊，
她日日夜夜盼着遮帕麻回还。

His power cannot be compared with mine;
No matter how wide the earth that Chye Mi Ma wove,
It's not wide enough for me to put my magic into good use.

"I will take charge of the sky and the earth.
Only the strongest one can be the king.
Whoever dares to stand in my way,
I will make him suffer and soon die.

"To kill or not to kill is up to me;
I don't care what others say.
East, west, south and north are all under my control.
Life and death are in my hands."

Sheep scattered by wolves
Would bleat in search of their master;
Birds scattered by the gale
Would tweet to find their companions.

Seeing the destruction of life,
Chye Mi Ma was as worried as ants on a hot pan.
Unable to defeat La Hong,
She had to wait day and night for Chye Hpa Ma's return.

第二折　水獭猫送信

遮帕麻南行的时候，
曾站在家门口，
指着南流的河水对遮米麻说：
“我就顺着这条河走。

“南边的天补好了，
我就叫河水倒着流，
让它回来报信，
你在家里把我等候。”

想起遮帕麻的留言，
遮米麻天天去到河边：
看滔滔的河水呵，
有没有倒流回来。

早上跑三转，
下午跑三转，
晚上跑三转，
一天跑九转。

Canto 2　An Otter Sending a Message

Before he went south,
Chye Hpa Ma stood by the door,
Pointing to the river that runs south, and said to Chye Mi Ma:
"I will travel along this river.

"When the southern sky is mended,
I will tell the river to run backwards
To send you a message.
You just wait for me at home."

Thinking of what Chye Hpa Ma had said to her,
Chye Mi Ma went to the river every day
To see whether the river
Was flowing backwards.

Three times she went to check in the morning.
Three times she went to check in the afternoon.
Three times she went to check at night.
She checked nine times a day.

望着南去的流水，
遮米麻大声呼唤：
“清清的流水呀，
快快流到拉涅旦。

“请带个信给遮帕麻，
就说生灵遭祸殃，
魔王霸占了天地，
叫他赶快把家还。”

看着滚滚南流水，
总是不见它折头。
遮米麻两眼都望穿，
心里又添一层愁。

向着南边的天，
遮米麻大声地呼唤：
“遮帕麻啊遮帕麻，
你要快快把家还。”

南边的天空空荡荡，
听不到一声回响；
南天上的云彩停下了脚步，

Looking at the river flowing southwards,
Chye Mi Ma cried out:
"Clean and clear water,
Please flow fast to La-nye Tan.

"Please send a message to Chye Hpa Ma,
And tell him that all creatures are suffering miserably.
The devil has taken over the world,
And ask him to return home quickly."

Watching the water rolling southwards
And never reversing its course,
Chye Mi Ma strained her vision watching for Chye Hpa Ma,
Bearing one more worry in her mind.

Looking toward the southern sky,
Chye Mi Ma cried out:
"Chye Hpa Ma! Chye Hpa Ma!
You must make haste to return home."

The southern sky was empty;
There was no reply;
The clouds in the south had stopped floating.

信儿怎么传得到南方？

忽然看见两条狗，
正在河里游，
遮米麻立刻跑上去，
站在河边请求：

“小狗啊小狗，
赶快顺水游，
踩着遮帕麻的脚印走，
叫他回来把妖魔收。”

两只小狗摇摇头：
“拉涅旦山高路难走，
从头到尾几千里，
不知要跑到什么时候？

“腊訇把我们赶下水，
空长四脚不能走；
叫我送信我高兴，
要游几千里怎能忍受？

“路上饿了没吃的，

How could she send a message to the south?

Suddenly she saw two dogs
Swimming in the river.
Chye Mi Ma immediately ran up to them.
She stood by the river and pleaded:

"Dear dog, dear dog,
Take a quick swim along the river.
Follow the footsteps of Chye Hpa Ma,
And tell him to come back and defeat the demon."

The two dogs shook their heads.
"There are high mountains and difficult paths on the way to La-nye Tan.
There are thousands of miles from beginning to end.
When on earth could we get there?

"La Hong drove us into the water.
Though we have four legs, we cannot walk.
We would be glad to help send the message,
But how can we swim thousands of miles?

"There would be nothing to eat on the way.

碰上老虎要丢命，
遮米麻啊，我们实在害怕，
还是让我们留在这里。”

听了狗的话，
遮米麻急得直搓手：
信儿送不到，
妖魔怎么收？

忽然又见两只鸡，
漂在河里顺水流，
遮米麻赶快跑上去，
站在河边请求：

“小鸡啊小鸡，
赶快往南游，
踩着遮帕麻的脚印走，
叫他回来把妖魔收。”

小鸡摇头开口讲：
“太阳我能叫出山，
但远在南边的遮帕麻呀，
我无法把他叫回来。

If we meet a tiger, we surely will lose our lives.
Chye Mi Ma, we are really afraid!
Please let us stay here."

After hearing what the dogs said,
Chye Mi Ma wrung her hands anxiously:
If the message cannot be sent out,
How can the demon be defeated?

Suddenly she saw two chickens
Floating in the river.
Chye Mi Ma ran up to them quickly.
She stood by the river and pleaded:

"Chicken, chicken,
Please swim southwards quickly.
Follow the footsteps of Chye Hpa Ma,
And tell him to come back and defeat the demon."

The chicken shook their heads and said:
"We can call the sun from behind the mountains,
But as Chye Hpa Ma is staying far to the south,
We cannot call him back.

“腊訇把我赶下水，
不许上岸回窝里；
派我送信我高兴，
可惜我打湿了的翅膀不会飞。

“路上饿了没吃的，
碰上野猫更倒霉，
遮米麻啊，我们实在没本领，
还是让我们留在这里。”

听了小鸡的话，
遮米麻急得流眼泪：
信儿送不到，
遮帕麻何时才得归？

有只小獭猫，
自自在在漂水上：
泅水它比鱼灵活，
上岸跑得比狗快。

腊訇把它撵下水，
吃鱼吃虾饿不倒；

"La Hong drove us into the water,
And forbid us to go ashore and return to our nests;
It would be our pleasure to send the message,
But it's a pity that our wet wings can no longer fly.

"There would be nothing to eat on the way.
It will be bad luck if we should encounter a wildcat.
Chye Mi Ma, we do not have that ability.
Please let us stay here."

After hearing what the chicken said,
Chye Mi Ma anxiously wept:
If the message cannot be sent out,
How can the demon be defeated?

There was a little otter
Floating freely in the water:
In the water it could swim better than a fish.
On the shore it could run faster than a dog.

La Hong drove it into the water,
But it ate fish and shrimps and did not starve;

腊訇把它赶上山，
打个山洞能安家。

它看见遮米麻啊，
坐在岸边淌眼泪，
便张开笑脸走上来，
说几句宽心话来安慰：

“遮米麻啊好奶奶，
什么事情想不开？
有了难处告诉我，
有什么事情我来帮忙。”

遮米麻听了多欢喜，
抱起獭猫把泪揩净。
指着太阳骂腊訇，
望着南方直叹气：

“你看这天不像天，
你看这地不像地，
世界成了这个样，
叫我怎么不着急？

La Hong drove it up to the mountain,
But it could dig a cave and made a home.

As it saw Chye Mi Ma
Sitting on the shore weeping,
It came up with a smile on the face
And said a few words of comfort:

"Chye Mi Ma, my dear granny,
What are you taking so hard?
If you have a problem, tell me.
I'll help you with anything."

How glad Chye Mi Ma was to hear this!
She picked up the otter and wiped away her tears.
Pointing to the sun, she cursed La Hong.
Looking south, she sighed:

"You see, the sky is not what it was,
And the earth doesn't look like before.
Since the world has become such a world,
How can I stay calm?

“只有叫回遮帕麻，
才能除掉魔王。
信要送到拉涅旦，
只好派你前往。

“小獭猫你听仔细，
我的嘱托莫忘记——
跑在山上别贪玩，
游在水里莫大意。

“顺着遮帕麻的脚印走，
快快赶到拉涅旦去，
喊回天公，重整天地，
那时我招你作女婿。”

小獭猫点点头：
“奶奶不用愁，
信儿我去送，
不见到天公不折头！”

这个可爱的水獭猫，
不怕水深山高，
朝着遥远的拉涅旦，

"Only when Chye Hpa Ma is called back
Can the demon be gotten rid of.
The message has to be sent to Chye Hpa Ma,
And I'll have to send you there.

"Listen carefully, little otter.
My instructions must not be forgotten—
Don't play in the mountains;
Don't be careless when swimming in the water.

"Follow the footprints of Chye Hpa Ma,
And hurry to La-nye Tan.
Call back the father of the sky to restore the sky and the earth,
And you will be my son-in-law."

The little otter nodded,
"Granny, you need not worry.
I'll send the message,
And I won't return before I see the father of the sky!"

This lovely otter
Was afraid of neither deep water nor high mountains.
Towards distant La-nye Tan

睁大眼睛拼命跑。

翻了九十九座山，
过了九十九条河，
肚子空了不知饿，
嗓子干了不知渴。

这个机灵的水獭猫，
不知跑了多少路程，
肉跑掉了九斤，
皮磨破了九层。

身上的毛结成了疙瘩，
头上沾满了灰尘，
嗓子干得说不出话，
肚子饿得头发昏。

忽然看到一片椰子林，
林中有个小村庄，
村外一眼井，
井水清汪汪。

水獭猫想进村，

It ran hard with its eyes wide open.

It had climbed over ninety-nine mountains;
It had crossed ninety-nine rivers;
It did not notice that its stomach was empty,
And it did not notice that its throat was dry.

Nobody knew how many miles
It had run:
More than nine *jin* of weight had been lost;
Nine layers of skin had been worn out.

The hair on its body got tangled into knots.
Dust was all over its head.
Its throat was too dry to speak.
It got so hungry that it felt dizzy.

Suddenly it saw a coconut grove,
In which there was a small village.
Outside the village there was a well,
Whose water was clean and clear.

The otter wanted to enter the village,

去把遮帕麻打听；
可身上脏得不像样，
邋里邋遢不好见人。

看着清汪汪的水，
水獭猫纵身跳下井：
先喝水，后洗澡，
又是翻身又打滚。

干渴全解了，
皮毛洗亮了，
身上凉快了，
却把井水搅浑了。

水獭猫跳到草地上，
放平身子烤太阳。
一路奔跑太劳累，
躺在地上睡得香。

寨门“吱呀”响，
走出一个挑水的女人：
上坡好像柳迎风，
下坡好像风送云。

To inquire about Chye Hpa Ma;
But it was really so dirty all over,
And it was too dirty to meet anyone.

Seeing the clear water,
The otter jumped into the well:
It drank water first and then took a bath,
Turning and rolling over.

Its thirst was gone;
Its fur was shining;
It felt cool,
But the water was muddied.

The otter jumped onto the grass
And lay flat to enjoy the sunshine.
Running all the way, it felt so tired,
And slept soundly on the ground.

The village gate was opened.
Stepping out of it was a woman carrying water,
Who went uphill as lightly as a willow against the wind,
And moved downhill as swiftly as the wind sending clouds.

她的头发比燕子毛还黑，
她的脸比鹭鸶毛还白，
她牙齿比石榴籽还密，
这个美人就是桑姑尼。

她来到井边，
刚刚舀起一桶水来
就吓了一大跳：
清清的井水变成了泥浆！

阿公阿祖留下话，
井水变浑地要塌。
桑姑尼水也不敢挑，
急急忙忙转回家。

忽然看见水獭猫，
呼呼大睡正打鼾。
定下心来仔细看，
獭猫身上的水汽还不干。

桑姑尼心里直冒火，
张开嘴巴大声骂：

Her hair was darker than a swallow's.
Her face was whiter than a crane's plumage.
Her teeth were thicker than pomegranate seeds.
This beauty was the salt lady Sang-gu Ni.

She came to the well.
Hardly had she scooped up a bucket of water
When she was startled:
The clean well water had turned into mud!

Our forefathers had left a message:
The earth would collapse when the well became muddy.
Sang-gu Ni did not dare carry the water
And hurried home.

Suddenly she saw the otter
Snoring in its sleep.
She took a closer look
And saw the otter was still wet.

Sang-gu Ni flew into rage.
She shouted:

“哪里来的野东西！”
提起扁担就要打。

水獭猫惊醒了，
一骨碌跳起来，
躲开桑姑尼的扁担，
边说话边揉眼：

“我是北方来的客呀，
遮米麻派我来找遮帕麻。
妖魔腊訇作乱了，
这音信要当面告诉他。”

听说来找遮帕麻，
桑姑尼的眼睛亮了，
桑姑尼的心里乐了，
高高举起的扁担放下了。

“遮帕麻就住在我家，
跟着我就能见到他。
今天他去打麂子，
太阳落山才回家。

"You dirty thing!"
She raised her shoulder pole to beat the otter.

The otter was awakened
And all at once jumped up.
Ducking the shoulder pole,
It rubbed its eyes and said:

"I am a visitor from the north.
Chye Mi Ma sent me here to find Chye Hpa Ma.
The demon La Hong has staged an insurrection.
And I must give Chye Hpa Ma this message in person."

Hearing this,
Sang-gu Ni's eyes lit up.
She was so happy
That her raised pole was lowered.

"Chye Hpa Ma lives in my house.
Follow me and you will see him.
Today he has gone deer hunting,
And he won't come home before the sun sets.

“你是北方来的客，
我回家给你泡茶。
肚子饿了不用愁，
我家里有鱼也有虾。”

水獭猫心里欢喜，
跟着盐婆就走。
刚要跨进门，
一跳跳到桑姑尼的肩头。

“奶奶奶奶我害怕，
我的身上有股怪味道，
你家的猎狗恶，
闻到骚味会把我咬。”

“小獭猫，你别害怕，
猎狗撵山不在家；
回头你就躲在屋梁上，
等我拴好猎狗再下来。”

遮帕麻打猎一整天，
麂子的影子都不见，
辛辛苦苦无收获，

"Since you are a visitor from the north,
I'll go home and make you some tea.
Don't worry if you're hungry.
I have fish and shrimps in my house."

The otter's heart rejoiced,
And it followed the salt lady.
At the door,
It suddenly jumped onto Sang-gu Ni's shoulder.

"Granny, I am scared.
I have a strong scent.
Your hound must be ferocious,
And the foul smell will make it bite me."

"Little otter, don't be afraid.
The hound is away chasing prey in the mountains;
You hide yourself on the ridge purlin when it comes back,
And wait above there till I tie the hound."

Chye Hpa Ma had hunted all day long,
But there was no sign of any deer.
Pain without gain,

两手空空下山来。

半路碰上瓢泼大雨，
从头到脚都淋遍，
泥浆溅在身上，
愁苦挂在脸上。

到家赶走了兵和将，
烧起火塘烤衣裳。
湿柴点火火不燃，
不见火苗只冒烟。

黑烟腾腾冲屋梁，
熏坏了梁上的水獭猫：
又是咳嗽又流泪，
一边叫喊一边跳。

遮帕麻看见水獭猫，
抓起棒棒就要打：
“满山找不着一根麂子毛，
想不到野物自己送到家！”

吼声传进厨房里，

He came home empty-handed.

It was raining heavily on the way,
And he got wet from head to toe.
Mud splashed on his body,
And sorrow and distress showed on his face.

Arriving home, he sent away his attendants.
He started a fire to dry his clothes.
But the wet wood would not kindle;
There was no fire, just smoke.

Black smoke reached the beams,
And it irritated the otter who was up there:
Coughing and shedding tears,
It cried out and jumped.

When Chye Hpa Ma saw the otter,
He grabbed a big stick to hit it:
"There was no sign of a deer in the mountains.
Who can imagine there is a wild animal in the house!"

His shouting reached the kitchen.

急坏了正在做饭的桑姑尼：
“快住手，别动气，
它是北边来的小东西。”

听说水獭猫从家乡来，
遮帕麻的怒气顿时消。
连忙抱下小东西，
一面问好一面笑。

水獭猫跳上遮帕麻的肩膀，
咬着耳朵把音信传：
“腊訇乱世搅窝子，
遮米麻盼你快回还……”

第三折　遮帕麻回归

激怒了的大象，
会把竹林踏平；
惊人的消息呵，
撕碎了遮帕麻的心：

“一拃长的花蛇，
竟想吞下大象！

Sang-gu Ni, who was cooking, was shocked:
"Stop! Calm down!
It's a little thing from the north."

Hearing that the otter came from his hometown,
Chye Hpa Ma's anger subsided.
He quickly took the little thing down,
And said hello with a smile.

The otter jumped onto Chye Hpa Ma's shoulder,
And whispered the message to him:
"The demon La Hong has stirred up the world,
And Chye Mi Ma is looking forward to your quick return..."

Canto 3　Chye Hpa Ma Returning Home

An enraged elephant
Can flatten the bamboo forest;
The shocking news
Tore the heart of Chye Hpa Ma into pieces:

"A serpent of an arm's length
Should think of swallowing an elephant!

故乡的百姓正在遭殃，
我怎能不去救难？”

遮帕麻收拾行装要上路，
桑姑尼心里乱如麻。
她走上前来拉着他，
眼里泪水如雨下：

“遮帕麻呵遮帕麻，
拉涅旦哺育我长大，
要我离开这里哟，
心里实在放不下。

“离开抱我长大的阿爹，
离开奶我长大的阿妈，
离开我朝夕相处的兄妹，
我的心啊似刀剐。

“砍下我的两腿留在家吧，
免得爹妈和兄妹常牵挂；
可是归途九千里，
没有腿怎么把山爬？

The people of my hometown are suffering.
How can I not go to their rescue?"

Chye Hpa Ma packed up and got ready to depart.
Sang-gu Ni was utterly upset and in a state of confusion.
She came up to him and held his arm.
Tears were in her eyes.

"Dear Chye Hpa Ma,
I was born and grew up in La-nye Tan;
I can't bring myself
To part from it.

"Saying farewell to my dad who raised me up,
Separating from my mom who gave me milk,
And leaving my siblings,
Would break my heart.

"I want to cut off my legs and leave them at home,
So that my parents and siblings would not miss me so much.
But the return journey is nine thousand miles.
How could I climb the mountains without legs?

“砍下我的双手留在家吧，
免得爹妈和兄妹常牵挂；
可是路程九千里，
没有手怎么抱娃娃？

“砍下我的脑壳留在家吧，
免得爹妈和兄妹常牵挂；
可是没有脑壳不能活哟，
怎能跟你回去熬盐巴？

“双腿不能不留着，
双手不能不留着，
脑壳不能不留着，
遮帕麻呵还是留下吧！”

听说遮帕麻要回家，
拉涅旦的百姓也苦苦留他：
“遮帕麻呵你不能走，
这里就是你的家。

“我们离开了你，
就会像冬天的树丫；
我们离开了你，

"I want to cut off my hands and leave them at home,
So that my parents and siblings would not miss me so much.
But the return journey is nine thousand miles.
How could I hold a baby without hands?

"I want to cut off my head and leave it at home,
So that my parents and siblings would not miss me that much.
But I will be dead without my head.
How could I go back with you to boil salt?

"I can't leave my legs behind.
I can't leave my hands behind.
I can't leave my head behind, either.
So please stay, Chye Hpa Ma!

Hearing that Chye Hpa Ma would return to his home,
The people of La-nye Tan also tried to make him stay:
"You cannot leave, Chye Hpa Ma,
Your home is here.

"Without you,
We would be like tree branches in winter;
Without you,

就会像没有露珠的小草。”

十人围不过的大榕树，
狂风也不能把它摇动；
百姓的眼泪哟，
却使遮帕麻感动：

“你们诚心挽留，
我万分感激；
你们对我的爱戴，
我永远铭记。

“我跟北方、南方的百姓，
都心连着心，
是去还是留，
看天意来定。

“现在就派兵将去狩猎，
不打老虎也不打狐狸；
专撵山老鼠，
看它的行踪测天意。

“老鼠出新洞、进旧洞，

We would be like grass without dewdrops.

A gale cannot shake a banyan tree that is so big
For ten men to embrace it with their arms.
But the tears of the people
Moved Chye Hpa Ma.

"You ask me to stay,
And I'm grateful.
Your love for me
Will always be remembered.

"The people of the north and the south are both on my mind,
And our hearts are linked together;
Whether I am to leave or to stay,
Will depend on providence.

"Send men now to hunt.
They should hunt neither the tiger nor the fox.
They will follow a mountain rat
And see what happens.

"If the rat leaves a new hole and enters an old one,

天意要我回北方除魔王；
老鼠出旧洞、进新洞，
天意要我留在南方。”

兵将打猎回家来，
欢欢喜喜地讲：
“老鼠出新洞、进旧洞，
天意要你去除魔王。”

遮帕麻提起赶山鞭，
点齐兵将就要启程，
拉涅旦的百姓拦路哭，
离别的泪水湿透了衣襟：

“要高飞的金孔雀呵，
不要忘记你栖息过的地方；
要离开我们的遮帕麻呵，
不要忘记你居住过的村庄。”

I am destined to go back to north to get rid of the demon.
If the rat leaves an old hole and enters a new one,
Then my fate is to stay in the south."

The soldiers and generals came back from hunting,
And told him exultantly:
"The rat came out of a new hole and went into an old one;
Your destination is to go and get rid of the demon."

Chye Hpa Ma lifted his whip,
And with the army all ready, he was about to set out.
And the people of La-nye Tan wept along the way.
The tears of parting soaked their skirts.

"The golden peacock that flies high,
Please don't forget where it once lived.
Dear Chye Hpa Ma, you are leaving us,
But please don't forget the village you once lived in."

第四部分 降妖除魔

Book 4 Defeating the Demon

大山压顶的时候，
要挺直腰杆；
大难临头的时候，
要咬紧牙关。

天最黑的时候，
千万不要慌张：
黑暗总有尽头，
东方就要升起太阳。

第一折　斗法

腊訇乱世三年，
大地闹了四年饥荒。
天底下没有一丝阴凉哟，
连大青树也都枯黄。

活着的百姓逃亡他乡，
死了的百姓堆满路旁；
专吃腐肉的乌鸦呵，
也伤心得眼泪汪汪。

天空飘过朵朵白云，

When the mountain falls upon you,
Stand up straight;
When disaster strikes you,
Grit your teeth and hang on.

When it is the darkest,
Don't panic;
The darkness has an end,
When the sun rises in the east.

Canto 1　A Battle of Magical Powers

La Hong had staged an insurrection for three years.
The earth had suffered from a famine for four years.
There was no shade under the sky,
Even the great banyan trees' leaves withered and turned yellow.

Those who survived fled their homeland.
Dead bodies piled up along the road;
Even the crows that ate carrion
Felt sad, tears welling up in their eyes.

White clouds floating in the sky

传来了下雨的消息；
聪明伶俐的水獭猫哟，
带来了遮帕麻回归的音信。

遮帕麻回到故乡，
遮米麻到山脚迎接。
不等天公进家门，
便滔滔倾诉心中的苦和恨：

“你看天上挂着一个假太阳，
使这里只有白天没有夜晚，
绿苗被烧焦，池水成泥塘，
魔王造下的罪孽说不完。

“腊訇这个大妖魔，
有兵有将会神通，
蝎子毒蛇没有他毒，
豺狼虎豹没有他凶。”

遮帕麻心里怒火烧，
一跳九丈高：
“妖精腊訇实在可恶，
不把他杀掉恨难消！”

Brought the good news of rain;
And the clever otter
Brought the news of the return of Chye Hpa Ma.

Chye Hpa Ma was approaching his homeland,
And Chye Mi Ma went to meet him at the foot of the mountain.
The moment she saw him,
She poured out all her heart's bitterness and sorrow.

"This is a fake sun you see in the sky,
Because of it there are only days but no nights here.
The green shoots have been scorched and the lakes have become muddy ponds.
No words can describe the crimes that the demon has committed.

"The demon La Hong
Controlled soldiers and generals, with magic powers.
Poisonous scorpions and venomous snakes are inferior to him.
Wolves, tigers and leopards are no worse than him."

Chye Hpa Ma's anger was burning within him,
And He jumped ninety feet high:
"The demon La Hong is truly abominable.
My hatred will not subside until he is killed!"

遮帕麻挥起赶山鞭，
鞭响似雷炸；
他要马上和魔王打仗，
召来了所有的兵马。

可又转念一想：
“两只老虎打架，
会揉伤田里的禾苗，
不能让战争把百姓糟蹋。”

举起的赶马鞭又轻轻放下，
集合的兵马又解散回家：
“在腊訇喝水的河里撒毒药，
那才是一个好办法。”

遮米麻一听连忙制止：
“遮帕麻呵你想的不妥当。
没有水，生灵怎么生活？
毒药不能撒水上。”

遮帕麻想了想说：
“不撒水里撒山上。

Chye Hpa Ma cracked his whip.
The sound of which was just like thunder.
He wanted to fight the devil at once,
And summoned all his soldiers and horses.

Then he had a second thought:
"When two tigers fight,
The crops in the field are crushed.
We must not launch a war that will hurt the people."

The raised whip was put down gently.
The assembled troops were dismissed and went home:
"Sprinkle poison in the river where the demon La Hong drinks.
That's a great idea."

Hearing this, Chye Mi Mai quickly stopped him:
"Chye Hpa Ma, that is not right.
How can the creatures live without water?
You can't poison the water."

Chye Hpa Ma thought for a moment and said:
"Then I shall spread poison over the mountains.

野果山菜都沾着毒，
腊訇吃了烂肝肠。”

遮米麻又劝告：
“山上动物万万千，
即使把妖魔毒死了，
无辜生灵也要受牵连。”

遮帕麻急得团团转：
“那还有什么好主张？”
遮米麻早有主意在心头：
“莫着急，先去跟腊訇交朋友。

“交了朋友再斗法，
瞅准时机好下手；
再烈的火也克不过水，
作乱的妖魔定能收。”

遮帕麻来到腊訇家，
魔王翻翻白眼不说话，
一副鬼相，满脸怒气，
不让坐也不倒茶。

Wild fruits and vegetables will become poisonous.
La Hong's liver and intestines will rot after he eats them."

Chye Mi Ma advised him:
"There are thousands of animals on the mountains;
Even if you can poison the demon,
Innocent living beings will also be affected."

Chye Hpa Ma got agitated and fussed about:
"What good idea is there?"
Chye Mi Ma had an idea in her mind:
"Don't worry. Go and make friends with the demon first."

"Friends first, fight later.
When the time is right;
No fire can defeat water.
The demon that makes trouble must be defeated."

Chye Hpa Ma came to the demon La Hong's house.
Rolling his eyes, the demon glared at him and said nothing.
Wearing a ghostly angry face,
He offered the guest neither a seat nor tea.

遮帕麻开口笑笑，
说出话来像蜜甜：
“从今以后交朋友，
不知你愿不愿？”

腊訇说话口水溅：
“要交朋友我为大，
天地归我管，
事事要听我的话。”

遮帕麻说：
“我们来比智斗法，
你要赢了就尊你为大，
我要胜了我就管天下。”

魔王没有话讲，
两个相邀到山前。
山凹里有棵花桃树，
枝繁叶茂花儿鲜。

腊訇上前去，
念了一串咒语，
又掐动手指头，

Chye Hpa Ma grinned.
He uttered words as sweet as honey:
"Let's make friends from now on,
Shall we?"

Saliva flew out when La Hong spoke:
"I will be the one to have the say if we make friends;
The world must be under my control,
And you must obey me in every way."

Chye Hpa Ma said:
"Let's have a contest of magical powers.
If you win, I will listen to you;
If I win, I will take control of the world."

The demon agreed.
They came to the foot of the mountain.
In the hollow there was a peach tree,
Which flourished, having many branches, leaves and flowers.

La Hong went up to the peach tree.
He uttered an evil spell
And pinched his fingers.

桃枝顿时叶蔫花枯。

他张开血口哈哈大笑，
洋洋得意地自夸：
“生灵死活我掌握，
谁的神通还能比我大？”

遮帕麻说：
“腊訇且莫夸，
谁有真本领，
要让枯枝再发芽。”

腊訇连连摇头：
“枯枝怎能再发芽？
枯花怎能再开放？
起死回生我无法。”

遮帕麻念动咒语，
又端来一碗泉水，
含一口清水喷花桃，
一眨眼工夫雨霏霏。

花桃重吐新芽，

The leaves and flowers on the peach tree branches withered at once.

He opened his fierce-looking mouth and laughed,
Boasting triumphantly:
"I control the life and death of all creatures.
Whose power is greater than mine?

Chye Hpa Ma said:
"La Hong, don't you boast.
The one who has the real ability
Can make the dead branches bud again."

La Hong shook his head repeatedly:
"How can a dead branch bud again?
How can the dead flowers bloom again?
I can't bring what is dead back to life."

Chye Hpa Ma uttered the words of a spell,
And then brought a bowl of spring water.
He sprayed a mouthful of water over the dead branches and flowers.
I in an instant,it rained.

The peach tree sprouted again.

枝头再开百花；
腊訇脸色像黄蜡，
目瞪口呆变成了哑巴。

第二折　斗梦

腊訇不服气，
又打鬼主意：
“今日斗法不算数，
明日斗梦比高低。

“做了好梦交好运，
做了恶梦不吉利。
谁该坐天下，
梦中看天意。”

遮帕麻上山顶，
腊訇下山箐。
各做各的梦，
约定明日到山腰谈梦境。

遮帕麻准时到山腰，
心里高兴脸带笑；

Hundreds of flowers bloomed again on the branches;
La Hong's face turned sallow.
He was dumbfounded and dumb.

Canto 2　A Battle of Dreams

La Hong was unconvinced,
And he got another idea:
"Today's battle will not count;
Tomorrow we will have another contest to see who is superior.

"A good dream predicts good luck,
While a bad dream foretells bad luck.
The one who will take control of the world
Will be determined by providence in our dreams."

Chye Hpa Ma went up to the top of the mountain,
While La Hong went down into the valley.
Each went on to dream his own dream,
After deciding to talk about their dreams on the mountainside the next day.

Chye Hpa Ma arrived at the mountainside punctually,
Smiling with pleasure;

腊訇垂头丧气，
心中像火烧。

遮帕麻说：
“我梦见太阳红彤彤，
山中泉水照人影，
树叶树枝青葱葱。”

腊訇有气无力地说：
“我梦见山顶黑乎乎，
箐沟流出黄泥水，
枯树枯枝光秃秃。”

遮帕麻做好梦，
腊訇做恶梦，
腊訇又输了，
遮帕麻又赢了。

腊訇耍赖说：
“昨天的梦不算数。
我上山顶你下箐，
再梦一回定输赢。”

La Hong was downcast,
As if there was a fire burning inside him.

Chye Hpa Ma said:
"I dreamed of the glowing red sun,
Spring water on the mountain was crystal clear,
And the leaves and branches were quite green.

La Hong said feebly:
"I dreamed of the dark top of the mountain.
Yellow muddy water flowed out of the valley,
And the dead trees and dead branches were bare."

Chye Hpa Ma had a good dream,
But La Hong had a nightmare.
La Hong lost again,
And Chye Hpa Ma won again.

La Hong said shamelessly:
"Yesterday's dream cannot count.
I will go up the mountain and you go down into the valley.
We will dream again to decide on the outcome."

遮帕麻点点头：
“再比一次也不怕。”
腊訇上了山顶，
遮帕麻来到山下。

第二天清早，
腊訇来找遮帕麻，
脸孔阴沉沉，
说话结结巴巴：

“我梦中不见太阳面，
只见山崩地倒塌，
满山枯藤挂老树，
浑水泥浆淌山洼。”

遮帕麻说：
“我梦见太阳亮堂堂，
绿树枝头喜鹊叫，
洼里泉水清汪汪。”

腊訇又输了，
脸色难看，像死了爹娘，
勉强答应交朋友，

Che Hpa Ma nodded:

"I have no objection to competing one more time."

La Hong went up to the top of the mountain,

And Chye Hpa Ma went down to the foot of the mountain.

Early the next morning,

La Hong came to visit Chye Hpa Ma,

His face was somber,

And spoke in a stammering way:

"The sun was not in my dream.

There were landslides.

Dead vines hung on the old trees.

Muddy water and mud ran down the mountain."

Chye Hpa Ma said:

"I dreamed of the shining sun.

The magpies were chirping in the branches of the green trees,

And the springs in the hollows were clean and clear."

La Hong lost again.

His face took on a ghastly expression as if he was attending his parents' funeral.

Reluctantly he agreed to make friends,

再也不说要尊他为王。

第三折　智伏腊訇

遮帕麻和腊訇交了朋友，
胸中有了战胜魔王的计谋，
回家提上赶山鞭，
高高兴兴往山上走。

白菌子红菌子撒入松林，
甜鸡纵香鸡纵撒在山头，
砍棵竹子抬回家，
编成竹筐和竹篓。

雷雨过后出鸡纵，
遮米麻拾回一满篓；
桑姑尼生火来烹煮，
加了盐，调了油。

送碗香喷喷的鸡纵给腊訇，
让他美味下米酒。
鸡纵香，米酒甜，
腊訇吃了直点头：

And never again insisted on being the king.

Canto 3　Subduing La Hong

Chye Hpa Ma succeeded in making friends with La Hong.
With a plan in his mind to defeat the devil,
He went back home for his whip,
And then went cheerfully up the hill.

White mushrooms and red mushrooms were scattered in the pine forest,
And sweet Jizong mushrooms were scattered on the hilltop;
He chopped down a bamboo tree and carried it home,
And he wove a big bamboo basket and also a small one.

After the thunderstorm and rain mushrooms sprang up,
And Chye Mi Ma picked up a full basket.
Sang-gu Ni made a fire and cooked the mushrooms,
Adding to the dish some salt and oil.

Chye Hpa Ma gave La Hong a bowl of delicious Jizong mushrooms
And told him that the delicious dish could go with his rice wine.
Jizong mushroom dish was tasty and rice wine was sweet;
La Hong was satisfied and nodded:

“美味鸡坳甜透心，
这样的好东西哪里有？
遮帕麻呵快快告诉我，
有福同享才算好朋友。”

遮帕麻真高兴，
凶恶的腊訇已上钩：
“爱吃只管上山采，
这种美味遍山有。”

遮帕麻提起赶山鞭，
拔脚就往山上走，
踏遍山头和山沟，
撒下毒菌“鬼见愁”。

遮米麻左肩挎竹筐，
遮米麻右肩挎竹篓，
去约腊訇家的小妖精：
“想吃鸡坳跟我走。”

遮米麻拾到毒菌放进竹筐，
遮米麻拾到鸡坳放进竹篓；

"The delicious mushroom dish was so satisfying;
Where did you find such a good thing?
Do tell me, Chye Hpa Ma.
Good friends should share happiness and good fortune."

Chye Hpa Ma was so happy;
The fierce demon La Hong had been hooked.
"If you love to eat them, just go up the mountain and pick them.
Delicious mushrooms are all over the mountains."

Chye Hpa Ma lifted his whip,
And immediately left and went up the mountain,
He went across every corner of the mountain and the ravine,
And scattered poisonous mushrooms wherever he passed.

The big basket was slung across her left shoulder,
The small one hung on her right shoulder,
Chye Mi Ma went to visit La Hong's little demon:
"Follow me if you want mushrooms."

Chye Mi Ma picked up the poisonous mushrooms and put them in the big basket.
Chye Mi Ma picked up edible mushrooms and put them in the small basket.

竹筐眼大装不住，
漏了一地“鬼见愁”。

小妖精拾起毒菌说：
“你的筐子漏呀，老奶奶！”
遮米麻装作慷慨的样子：
漏在地上的你只管顺手捡。”

遮米麻拾了一背甜鸡㙡，
小妖精捡了一背“鬼见愁”。
各自回到各的家，
腊訇见了口水直流。

等不得菌子煮熟，
腊訇就张开血盆大口，
一阵狼吞虎咽，
连渣带汤吃了个够。

腊訇吃了“鬼见愁”，
肚子疼得冷汗流，
倒在地上直打滚，
好像一万只老虎在吼。

The holes in the big basket were so big

That the poisonous mushrooms fell out and spread on the way.

The little demon picked up the poisonous mushrooms and said:

"Your big basket has holes, Granny!"

Chye Mi Ma pretended to be generous:

"You can just pick them up if they fall to the ground."

Chye Mi Ma picked up a basket of sweet Jizong mushrooms,

The little demon picked up a bag of poisonous ones.

Then they returned home.

La Hong's mouth was watering when he saw the mushrooms.

Before the mushrooms were well-cooked,

La Hong opened his big mouth

And wolfed down Everything,

Including the soup and all the mushrooms.

The mushrooms La Hong ate were known as "ghost worriers".

His stomach ached and he sweated.

Falling and rolling on the ground,

He roared as if ten thousand tigers were roaring.

腊訇家的妖精三天不出门，
腊訇家的房顶三天不冒烟，
不知腊訇死硬了没有？
遮帕麻派水牛去查看。

水牛刚出门，
天热淌大汗，
泡在水塘里，
忘了去查看。

遮帕麻一气穿了牛鼻子，
牛脖子上把弯担架：
“活着去犁田，
死了剐干巴！”

又派黄牛去查看，
黄牛来到半路上，
看见一片甘蔗林，
贪吃又把差事忘。

遮帕麻气坏了，
瞪着眼睛骂：
“瘦时挨鞭抽，

La Hong's demons stayed at home for three days.
No smoke was seen from La Hong's kitchen for three days.
Had La Hong died?
Chye Hpa Ma sent a buffalo to have a look.

No sooner had the buffalo left the house
Than it felt hot and sweated.
It had a bath in a pond,
And forgot about its task.

Chye Hpa Ma got angry and pierced the buffalo's nose,
And he put a yoke around the buffalo's neck and cursed:
"Live to plow,
Die to be cut and made into dried beef!"

An ox was then sent to check it.
On the way, it saw a field of sugar cane
And started to eat,
Forgetting all about its task.

Chye Hpa Ma really got mad at it.
He scowled at the ox and cursed:
"You will get whipped when you are thin,

胖了用刀杀！”

又派马儿去查看，
马儿走进腊訇家，
看见一摊草，
只顾把滚打。

遮帕麻揪住马尾骂：
“让人骑着跑，
罚去驮东西，
鞍子背上架！”

召来两只小麻雀，
展翅飞到腊訇家，
看见魔王死硬了，
回来告诉遮帕麻。

喜讯乐坏遮帕麻，
高高兴兴对麻雀说道：
“饿了谷囤头上吃，
天黑就住屋檐下。”

又派两只小老鼠，

And get killed with a knife when you are fat!"

A horse was then sent to check it.
Arriving at La Hong's house,
The horse saw a pile of grass in the yard.
It did nothing but roll on the grass.

Chye Hpa Ma seized the horse's tail and shouted a curse:
"People will ride on you and make you run.
You will carry a load,
A saddle on back!"

Two little sparrows were summoned.
They spread their wings and flew to La Hong's house.
Seeing the demon's dead body,
They came back and reported it to Chye Hpa Ma.

The good news excited Chye Hpa Ma.
He happily said to the sparrows:
"When you get hungry, you will eat at the top of the grain bin.
In the evening, you will live under the eaves."

Two little mice were then sent to check it.

飞快跑到腊訇家，
老鼠闻见魔王尸臭了，
咬回两个手指甲。

消息喜坏遮帕麻，
高高兴兴对老鼠说道：
“谷囤米囤脚下吃，
墙脚打洞去安家。”

出来一只大苍蝇，
嗡嗡飞到腊訇家，
在魔王鼻孔耳孔里下子，
在魔王眼珠上搓脚。

飞回告诉遮帕麻，
遮帕麻对苍蝇说道：
“甑子头上你去吃，
饭桌上面任你抓。”

腊訇的尸体臭气冲天，
狗去咬他的心，
猪去拱他的肝，
七零八散，碎成万段。

They ran fast to La Hong's house,
Smelled the demon's dead body,
Bit off two of his fingernails and returned.

The good news excited Chye Hpa Ma.
He happily said to the mice:
"You will eat at the foot of the grain bin,
And you will dig a hole in the wall as your home."

There came a big fly,
Which buzzed to La Hong's house.
It laid its eggs in the demon's nose,
And rubbed its feet on the demon's eyes.

It flew back to report to Chye Hpa Ma,
Who said to the fly:
"You will have your food on the steamer;
You can eat the food on the table."

La Hong's dead body stank.
The dog bit his heart,
And the pig dug its nose into his liver,
Breaking his body into ten thousand pieces.

第四折　重整天地

腊訇凶狂野心大，
天理不容，自取身亡，
可他射上去的假太阳，
还散发着毒光。

森林还在冒着烟，
竹子还在倒着长；
山上的动物还在水里挣扎，
水里的鱼虾还困在山上。

遮帕麻拉开黄栗硬弓，
搭上九拿长的弩箭，
一箭射下假太阳，
天空不再喷毒焰。

天上出现了遮帕麻造的太阳，
天上出现了遮帕麻造的月亮，
太阳会出也会落，
月亮会升也会降。

Canto 4　Restoring the Sky and the Earth

La Hong was fierce and ambitious.
God forbid this and took away his life.
But the fake sun he shot up
Was still there giving out a toxic glow.

The forest was still smoking.
Bamboo trees were still growing upside down.
Terrestrial animals were still struggling in the water,
While fish and shrimps were still stranded on the mountain.

Chye Hpa Ma drew his bow made from a chestnut tree,
And with a nine arm-span arrow,
He shot down the fake sun,
So that the sky no longer gave out burning heat.

The sun made by Chye Hpa Ma reappeared in the sky.
The moon made by Chye Hpa Ma reappeared in the sky.
The sun could rise and set.
The moon could also rise and set.

遮帕麻挥舞赶山鞭，
把倒插的树木扶正，
把倒流的河水理顺，
把颠倒了的世界重新整顿。

水里的兽类放回山上，
山上的水族放回河里，
只有会打洞的穿山甲，
自愿留在山里。

遮帕麻甩动赶山鞭，
鞭树树成林，
鞭水水更清，
鱼儿回水鸟归林。

鱼儿回水得自由，
鸟儿归林传歌声，
英雄的遮帕麻呵，
理顺了阴阳挽救了生灵。

遮帕麻立下古老的规矩，
精心把世界管理。
百姓受苦他伤心，

Chye Hpa Ma wielded his whip.
He corrected the inverted trees.
He corrected the backward-running rivers.
He reorganized the upside-down world.

The terrestrial animals in the water were put back on the mountains.
The aquatic animals on the mountains were put back in the rivers.
Only the pangolins that could punch holes
Volunteered to stay in the mountains.

Chye Hpa Ma lashed his whip.
When the whip touched the trees, they turned into a forest;
When the whip touched the water, it became even clearer;
Fish returned to the water and birds returned to the forest.

Fish returned to the water to swim freely;
Birds returned to the forest to sing happily;
Our hero Chye Hpa Ma
Saved the creatures by puttingYin and Yang in order.

Chye Hpa Ma set up permanent rules,
And he managed the world carefully.
When the people suffered, he was grieved.

百姓安宁他欢喜。

他派三十个神兵守山头，
临走时对他们讲：
“见毒蛇就要拔出长刀，
对鬼怪决不能手软。”

他派三十员神将管村寨，
出发前一再对他们告诫：
“从今以后谁敢再作乱，
就跟腊訇同样下场！”

干涸了的池塘又流出清水，
逃出去的百姓又回到故乡；
烧光的草地又变绿，
枯死的鲜花又开放。

田里的谷子一年两次黄，
肥壮的牛羊满山岗；
大树高兴得招手，
河水高兴得歌唱。

最动听的调子是“俄罗”，

When they enjoyed a peaceful life, he was happy.

He stationed thirty divine soldiers on the mountains.
Before they left, he said to them:
"Draw your long knife at the sight of any viper,
And never be kind to ghosts or monsters."

He appointed thirty divine generals to guard the villages.
He told them again and again before they left:
"Whoever shall dare to make any further mischief,
La Hong's fate will also be his!"

The dry pond was full of water again.
The people who had fled returned to their homeland.
The burnt grass turned green again.
Dead flowers bloomed again.

The crops in the field ripened twice a year.
Fat cattle and sheep filled the hills.
The trees waved in delight.
The rivers sang cheerfully.

The sweetest tune is the "Eluo" tune.

最美丽的花朵是攀枝花；
唱一支“俄罗”歌颂遮帕麻，
采一朵攀枝花献给遮米麻。

阿昌的子孙呵，
这就是遮帕麻和遮米麻的故事，
你们要牢牢记在心里，
世世代代传唱不歇。

遮帕麻和遮米麻的故事，
像天一样久长；
要知故事的来历，
请问月亮和太阳。

遮帕麻和遮米麻的故事，
像大地一样长存不衰；
要问故事出自哪里？
阿昌心底是它的故乡。

The most beautiful flowers are the kapok flowers.
A song with the "Eluo" tune is sung in praise of Chye Hpa Ma.
A kapok flower is picked and offered to Chye Mi Ma.

Descendants of the Achang,
This is the story of Chye Hpa Ma and Chye Mi Ma.
You must remember this story,
And pass it on from generation to generation.

The story of Chye Hpa Ma and Chye Mi Ma
Is as long as the lifespan of the sky.
To understand where the story comes from,
You may ask the moon and the sun.

The story of Chye Hpa Ma and Chye Mi Ma
Has lasted as long as the earth.
Do you want to know where the story comes from?
Every Achang descendant has this story deep in his heart.

译后记

《遮帕麻与遮米麻》是阿昌族目前最完整、篇幅最长的创世史诗，同时又是一部原始宗教巫师的诵词，由巫师在祭祀祖宗、举行葬礼等重要场合向族人念诵。

诗中的主人公遮帕麻与遮米麻是阿昌族民间所信仰和崇奉的两个最大的善神，狩猎者祈求他们赐予猎物；出外的人祈求他们保佑平安；不会生育的祈求他们赐给子女；有全体村民参加的大型祭祀，也是祈求他们保佑来年风调雨顺、六畜兴旺、五谷丰登、人口平安。史诗中作为反面形象来描写的魔王腊訇，则是阿昌族原始信仰中一个最大的恶神。如果日常生活里发生了什么事故或疾病，被"活袍"（巫师）确认是触犯了腊訇，那就要杀羊宰猪，请活袍念经以禳解。

《遮帕麻与遮米麻》英译采用的是云南人民出版社2016年出版的汉语文本。史诗共有4个部分12章节，共1400多行，每4行作为1个小节，语言简洁、韵律灵活。翻译此书，译者尽可能地保持原文的语言特点，力求确保原诗语言及意境的双重再现。

杨慧芳

Translator's Afterword

Chye Hpa Ma and Chye Mi Ma is the most complete and longest creation epic of the Achang ethnic group. It is also recited by primitive religious sorcerers to the clansmen on important occasions such as during ancestor worship and funerals.

Chye Hpa Ma and Chye Mi Ma are the hero and heroine of the epic, respectively. They are considered to be the greatest god and goddess and worshiped by the Achang people in the world. Hunters pray to them for prey; travelers pray to them for safety; women suffering from infertility pray to them for children; at great rituals in which all the villagers are present and people pray to them for blessing, for fine weather, for flourishing animals, for good harvest, and for safe and peaceful lives in the coming year. La Hong, the demon described as the antagonist in the epic, is the most powerful devil in the primitive belief of the Achang people. When in daily life a bad accident happens or a disease attacks, if the huopao confirms that it is the result of offending La Hong, a pig or sheep will be slaughtered and sacrificed by the huopao to La Hong in return for peace.

The source text of this English translation is the Chinese version published in 2016 by Yunnan People's Publishing House. The epic is composed of 4 books with 12 cantos, 350 quatrains and 1400 lines. The language is concise and the rhyme is flexible. When translating this book into English, the translator did her utmost to keep the language features of the original text so as to ensure both the reproduction of the language and the artistic conception of the original epic.

Yang Huifang

译者简介

杨慧芳，云南师范大学外国语学院副教授。代表性译著为《景颇族文史画册》（云南民族出版社，2007）。课余时间和假期里喜欢从事社会公益工作，进行文学作品的翻译和文化交流工作，其中服务时间较长的机构项目为亚洲开发银行资助的联合国教科文组织广播剧创作、翻译和录制项目：《湄公河次区域山地民族地区艾滋病预防教育项目》。2004—2012年参与并完成了德宏景颇族、德宏傣族、西双版纳傣族、临沧佤族、凉山彝族等5个少数民族广播剧的英文翻译。

About the Translator

Yang Huifang is an associate professor of English in the School of Foreign Languages and Literature at Yunnan Normal University. Her recent translation publication is *Jingpo Historical & Cultural Photo Album* (Yunnan Nationality Publishing House, 2007). Her research interests focus on literary translation and cross-cultural communication. She worked in 2004–2012 as a coordinator, translator and interpreter on the ADB-funded UNESCO project *HIV/AIDS Prevention Education among Highland Peoples in Sub-Mekong Regions*, which consisted of five programs: *Jingpo Ethnic Program in Dehong, Dai Ethnic Program in Dehong, Dai Ethnic Program in Xishuangbanna, Wa Ethnic Program in Lincang* and *Yi Ethnic Program in Liangshan*.